FERAL NATION

Insurrection

ALSO BY SCOTT B. WILLIAMS

The Pulse
Refuge
Voyage After the Collapse
Landfall
Horizons
Enter the Darkness
The Darkness After
Into the River Lands
The Forge of Darkness
The Savage Darkness
Sailing the Apocalypse
On Island Time: Kayaking the Caribbean

ISBN-13: 978-1981484614
Cover photographs: Fotolia #141926281 © Getmilitaryphotos, Fotolia #100579897 © Stephan Orsillo
Cover & interior design: Scott B. Williams
Editor: Michelle Cleveland

FERAL NATION
Insurrection

Scott B. Williams
Feral Nation Series Book Two

This one is for Jeffrey,
a friend like no other.

One

ERIC BRANSON MOVED THE shift lever from neutral into forward and opened the throttle of the 50-horse Yamaha outboard just enough to push the skiff downriver at about five knots. Slow and easy was the ticket. Anything else would likely get the two of them cut to pieces by rifle fire.

"Are you sure we ought to do this? I don't like the looks of this at all," Jonathan said.

"It's a little too late to turn back now. I think we're committed. If we try to back out it's just going to look suspicious. We don't really have another option anyway. Just be cool and keep your hands where they can see them and they probably won't shoot you."

"Probably won't? Yeah, that makes me feel better!"

Eric Branson understood Jonathan's anxiety. The two of them were approaching the channel blockade at the mouth of the Caloosahatchee River near Fort Myers, Florida, staring down the barrels of nearly a dozen rifles while sitting there in an 18-foot skiff in the wide open. If this meeting went sideways, it was doubtful either of them would survive it. But negotiating for their passage was a matter of survival as well. Eric's father and his ex-wife and her family were just a few miles upriver, waiting aboard the 42-foot sailboat anchored mid-channel above the Interstate 75 bridge overpass. This blockade of steel barges moored across the mouth of the Caloosahatchee was the only thing standing between them and the Gulf of Mexico, and it represented the first of many obstacles Eric knew he must overcome in the next phase of his quest to find his daughter. Eric and Bart had deemed it far too risky to first approach the blockade in the schooner due to the potential risk of losing the boat and everything aboard, as well as compromising the safety of the crew. Eric and Jonathan would instead take that risk alone, so after getting an anchor down in a quiet stretch of the river with good visibility, the two of them went ahead in Bart's skiff.

Ever since he'd met the kid in his hidden camp in the mangroves near Jupiter Inlet, Eric found Jonathan game for most anything, even forays as dangerous as this one. He could have come here alone, but decided it might look better to those in charge of this operation if he was accompanied by a young man he could pass off as his son. Eric would tell them his own father was also aboard their bigger boat waiting, which was the truth. Shauna and her husband and stepson he would claim as his sister and her family, even though in reality she was his former wife. He thought it might make them all appear less threatening if they presented themselves as one extended family doing their best to survive hard times, now seeking to leave the dangers of Florida to set sail for someplace safer. And for the most part that was true, but whether or not it would matter depended on the nature of this blockade and those who had set it up and now manned it. Eric didn't know whether they were authorities of some sort, or just regular citizens that banded together to protect the water entrance to their city. He had to consider also that they might be among the bad element. Many of that ilk had taken advantage of the situation here in Florida in the aftermath of the hurricane, a natural disaster that finished a breakdown of law and order that had already begun months before it struck.

Because of this uncertainty, Eric knew that anything could happen now that they were within rifle range of the blockade. He'd left his own rifles aboard the schooner, knowing that if this *was* an official checkpoint of some kind, the weapons could get him and Jonathan arrested at best or shot on the spot at worst. The only weapon he had on him was his Glock 19, tucked away in the appendix position inside the waistband of his shorts in a minimalist holster, the grip well covered by the bottom of his T-shirt. The handgun wouldn't be spotted unless they were physically searched, and while that was always a possibility, Eric couldn't bring himself to come here completely unarmed. If he were indeed destined to die here today, he would have the means to take one or more of his killers with him.

Eric had cut the outboard throttle to idle as soon as they rounded the final bend and came within sight of the blockade. As he and Jonathan sat there drifting, nearly a half mile away, he put out a call on Channel 16 on his handheld VHF radio to announce his intentions, and was directed to continue his slow approach by the man that answered. At that point it would have still been possible to turn around and leave, but not now. They were already in rifle range, and besides, Eric Branson wasn't in the habit of waffling on decisions once they were made.

"It's gonna suck if we're just running into a trap, dude."

"There's no use worrying about something that hasn't happened yet. Just chill, man. We're just going to have a chat with these fellows, that's all. It's not like we're sneaking up on them in the dark or something. I don't think they'll just kill us for no reason."

"I hope you're right, man. I really do."

Eric said nothing else. His focus now was on the objective, and he steered with the outboard to the barge that one of the men was pointing to, directing him to pull alongside. There was a long line of them moored end to end across the river, secured against the gentle current by heavy chain rodes that disappeared into the dark waters to unseen anchors below. There was no room for any kind of sizable vessel to pass, although a skiff like the one they were in could probably slip between the barges in a couple of places with permission from the guards.

Now that they were within speaking distance, Eric doubted seriously that the men manning this blockade were officials. Most of them looked more like local commercial fisherman or other local tradesmen, certainly not military or even civilian law enforcement. That could be either good or bad, and Eric knew he was about to find out which momentarily. He greeted the nearest man standing over him on the deck of one of the barges as they drifted closer. The man was watching him and Jonathan closely, the AR-15 in his hands at low ready, but not pointed directly at them as they were already well covered by his companions. This one seemed to be in charge though, and seeing the radio clipped to his belt, Eric assumed he was the one he'd spoken with already. Eric's friendly greeting was ignored however, answered only with a sharp question:

"What is it you want to talk about?"

"Like I said on the VHF, my son and I are here to find out what this blockade is all about, and see if we might get permission to pass. We want to leave the river. We want access to the Gulf."

"In that? Where do the two of you plan to go exactly?"

"No, it's not just us. The rest of my family is upriver on our sailboat. We knew you had the river closed here, but we assume the purpose is to keep vessels out, rather than in. Is that right?"

"The purpose is for us to decide. That's what it's for. We haven't had anyone coming down the river lately wanting out. There's not many honest people still around that are thinking about boats, other than a few local folks we know. But we've had more than our share of looters coming in here from other places. That's why we closed the river. So where did you come from that your boat is upriver? And why are you just now wanting to leave?"

"My father lives upriver not far from Lake Okeechobee. He owns a small boatyard there and the boat was on the hard there for refit since back before all the trouble started in the spring. My son Jonathan and I brought my sister and her family over to my father's place to ride out the hurricane, and we've been holding out there while we worked on the boat to get it ready to relaunch. We've had problems with looters too, and we knew it was going to get too dangerous to stay. Now that the boat is ready, it's time for us to go. We came this way because we didn't think we'd be able to transit the waterway going east because of the locks and dams. And we needed to get to the Gulf coast anyway because we're planning to sail across to get my brother."

"Across the Gulf? It had better be a seaworthy boat, then. Just how big is it?"

"Forty-two feet, with a twelve-foot beam. She's built for bluewater."

"Well, the only way you can get a boat that size through here is if we move one of these barges completely out of the way, and that's a hell of a lot of trouble. How do we know this sailboat even belongs to you? How do we know that you and your son aren't looters too, and that you didn't steal it? Maybe you even killed the owners for it?"

Eric and Bart had already discussed the issue of ownership of the schooner, and what they were going to do about documentation. In a way, they *had* essentially stolen the schooner. The true owners were a retired Canadian couple living in Ontario who'd contracted with Bart to store their vessel in his yard in the off season when they went home after their annual winter cruises. But now that south Florida had been laid to waste by a catastrophic hurricane and the rest of the country was paralyzed by violence and shortages of fuel and other goods, all the boats in Bart's boatyard were abandoned indefinitely. He'd done his best to protect them from looters while he could, but now it was time to leave. Bart knew the owners of the vessel formerly known as *Tropicbird* would never return, and that he would never collect storage or service fees for it or any of the other vessels on his property. If they didn't take the boat best suited to their purposes, someone else would, or it would be looted and stripped and left there on the hard indefinitely. In the end, all that mattered now was survival, and Bart had agreed with Eric that they had to look out for themselves from this point forward. It had taken some extra work, but they had gotten rid of all traces of the original name and documentation of the custom-built schooner, and created a new identity borrowed from a similar-sized Coast Guard documented sailing vessel in Bart's yard named *Dreamtime*.

Dreamtime was a steel-hulled ketch that was in a sad state of neglect. Her hull was rusting away and the vessel would likely never be launched again even if not for recent events. The owner was far in arrears on his storage fees and wasn't coming back. No one else would miss her and no one would likely be comparing the fine details of design and hull materials in the current circumstances anyway. A casual inspection of the Canadian schooner's metal hull wouldn't reveal that it was built of aluminum, rather than steel, because every exposed surface was painted with two-part epoxy paint. The size and displacement were close enough for a match, and so it was that *Tropicbird* became *Dreamtime*. The Colvin schooner left Bart's boatyard with the new name and the hailing port of Stuart, Florida painted on her stern, as well as borrowed documentation papers and a carved number plate bolted to her main bulkhead. Bart was certain that it was good enough to fool most people they might encounter, and he and Eric doubted they would be subject to serious scrutiny by U.S. Coast Guard or customs and immigration agents anytime soon. These guys guarding their river blockade were apparently civilians and were unlikely to notice any discrepancy. Eric was confident of that when he replied to the man's question:

"It's a Coast Guard documented vessel. The original owner kept it stored in my father's boatyard, but when all the riots started happening he decided he wanted to sell it fast and get what he could out of it. All the paperwork is on board, showing that he signed it over to my father months before the hurricane hit. My father's done a lot of work on it since, and with my son and I helping, we just recently got it ready to go. The boatyard and his house on the river are no longer safe and it's only going to get worse. Like I said before, that's why we're all leaving."

"I don't know where you expect to go that's going to be much better. Things are not just bad in Florida, you know."

"So I've heard," Eric said. "We still feel better about taking our chances out there though than staying here."

"It's not up to me or any one of us to decide if we can open up this blockade. We do things here by committee decision. One thing I can tell you though, is that it's going to cost you. Moving one of the barges out of the way and then putting it back in place is a lot of work."

"I kind of figured it wouldn't be free," Eric said. "We can pay, as long as the price is reasonable."

"The price will have to be determined. Committee, like I said. I can tell you this though, in case you don't already know it: checks, plastic, folding money and all other such nonsense is off the table. You're going to have to pay with something that is still of use in the present circumstances. I'm sure you understand why."

Eric did understand why. He understood that promissory notes and credit had little value with the economy in ruin, and he also understood that those in control of necessary goods and services could demand their price in whatever form they wanted. In this case, these men were in control of navigation at the mouth of this river, and the only option was to pay what they asked or try and get through by force. The latter wasn't a realistic option at all, considering that there were several armed men watching them at the moment, and no doubt many more out of sight among the dozen or so commercial fishing vessels anchored just inside the blockade. But Eric was prepared to pay, and he had brought proof of that with him.

"Will this work?" Eric produced a small yellow coin from his pocket, holding it up in the sunlight where the man could get a good look at it. A half-ounce of gold was worth a lot more than Eric wanted to give these people, but he'd already discussed it with Bart. The next best commodity of real value they had to offer was firearms and ammunition, of which they had plenty, but Eric feared that disclosing the presence of those on board could open them up for trouble if this was an authorized blockade. He deemed it far safer to offer payment in gold. The amount could be negotiated, and the half-ounce and one-ounce Krugerrand and other coins he had could be easily cut into segments to yield smaller denominations if such were needed.

The man took the coin from Eric and examined both sides before passing it to his companions, who nodded approval upon having a look. "This will do for a deposit. Bring your sailboat on down here where we can see it and have your crew stand by on it over there." He pointed to an open area near the south side of the channel. "Then you come back alone in your boat and bring me another one of these for the balance. It'll take us a good hour to move one of these barges and just as long to put it back after you leave. We'll get started as soon as we have your full payment."

"That's robbery!" Eric said. "That's a half ounce of gold and I don't *have* another one. It was a gift my father received from a friend years ago."

"I know how much gold it is, but what it's worth now is different from what it might have been worth before. What I can tell you it's *not* worth though, is all the trouble and work required to let a boat that size through here. Maybe you'd better ask your old man again. He probably has a little collection of these stashed away somewhere that he forgot to tell you about."

Eric said nothing, even though he *did* have many more of the coins along with the larger one-ounce variety as well. The truth was that none of them were Bart's though. The gold was Eric's severance and bonus pay that he'd negotiated with his employer when he'd left his well-paid contracting work in Europe. But Eric wasn't prepared to give more of it to these thieves. It was clear that they weren't going to be satisfied with the single half-ounce coin though, so he made a counter offer.

"I'll tell you what. Hold the coin for a deposit, and when we get our sailboat through, we'll leave you this skiff instead. We probably shouldn't try to tow it at sea anyway, in case we run into bad weather. As you can see, it's a good rig with a perfectly good Yamaha outboard. It's easily worth more than two of those coins and it's certainly useful. It's registered to my father and he has the paperwork on it and I'm sure he'll sign it over."

Eric and Jonathan waited while the men whispered among themselves and finally, the one he'd given the coin to said they had an agreement. He would hold the coin until they returned and then take the skiff and outboard when the blockade was opened for the passage of the bigger boat. With that settled, Eric put the Yamaha back in gear and turned and sped upriver to get Bart and the others.

Two

"I HEAR A BOAT coming," Shauna said. "That was quick!"

Bart couldn't hear it at all, but that didn't surprise him in the least. His hearing wasn't what it used to be, but he trusted Shauna's was better and he saw that Andrew and Daniel noticed the sound too. The four of them were down below in the main cabin of the schooner, cleaning up the galley and doing some last minute organization, securing everything in the storage lockers in preparation for the upcoming offshore voyage. They expected at least a half hour wait while Eric and Jonathan ran downriver in the skiff to see what the deal was with the blockade.

"It's *too* quick," Bart said, as he got up and grabbed his M1-A. "They haven't even had time to get down there, much less down there and back."

He mounted the companionway steps and made his way to the deck, followed closely by Shauna. As soon as he was half way up the ladder, he could hear the motor too, and he knew it was bigger than the 50-horsepower Yamaha on his skiff. He was also quite certain the boat was approaching from *upstream*, rather then down. A minute later and he saw that he was right as a 20-foot center console fishing boat rounded the bend. There were two men aboard, and when the one at the helm saw the sailboat anchored there mid river, he immediately slowed and made a slight turn, steering straight for it. Bart glanced over his shoulder and saw that Shauna was standing there behind him, already zeroing in on the strangers with the binoculars she'd grabbed from the shelf over the Nav station.

"Can you tell anything about them?" Bart asked.

"They look like a couple of regular guys, I guess. No uniforms or anything. I don't see any weapons on them."

"That doesn't mean a thing though, and you know it," Bart said. He made it a policy to assume anyone he met was armed these days, either openly or concealed. It was foolish not to be, of course, but dangerous too if the rumors they'd heard were true about how the authorities in some areas were dealing with armed civilians. *Dreamtime* was certainly carrying plenty of weapons and ammo, and Bart could only hope that any law enforcement officers they encountered wouldn't search the boat before they could leave Florida. Once they were offshore on the high seas he hoped the schooner would be considered a sovereign vessel and not subject to local restrictions. That was all theoretical, of course, because no one knew to what extent laws had been changed or new ones created. It was a damned if you do, damned if you don't kind of situation, but they had certainly favored the 'if you do side' and were willing to accept the risks that entailed.

When he was fairly certain that the two men in the skiff were not law enforcement officers, but a potential threat approaching the schooner, Bart stepped up to the rail on the side nearest them, making sure they could see the rifle without brandishing it directly. He wanted them to understand that he was armed and ready to defend his ship and her crew, and apparently, it worked. Whatever the two men may have wanted, they seemed to have suddenly reconsidered. The helmsman made a sharp turn in the direction of the farthest bank, giving them as much room as possible before speeding up again and continuing downriver to wherever the two of them had been going. That was a huge relief as far as Bart was concerned, because the last thing he wanted to do was engage in a firefight while anchored here in the middle of a wide-open river with only his former daughter-in-law for backup. Daniel and Andrew still had no experience with firearms other than practicing safe handling. Neither had even fired live rounds, much less at targets that might shoot back. Bart knew Shauna could do her part, but still....

"What do you think they wanted?" she asked.

"Who knows? Maybe they thought they'd come over and ask if we had any extra supplies or something we could spare. Or maybe they were going to ask where we came from."

"Well whatever it was, they sure changed their minds, seeing you standing there looking like you would just as soon shoot them as not."

"Better that than encourage them to get too close. I hate sitting here in the open like this."

Bart turned to see Andrew step on deck, followed by his father.

"Who was it, Shauna?" Daniel asked.

"Just a couple of guys in a boat. They went on. I don't suppose they meant any harm."

Bart didn't know what to think of a fellow that would wait down below while his wife went out to greet a possible threat. Of course he wasn't surprised by it now after getting to know the man over the course of several weeks. Daniel Hartfield simply wasn't cut out for the dangers of the harsh new reality in which he found himself suddenly immersed. It was a wonder he was here on board the boat at all, after all the arguing back and forth with Shauna about what they should do next. Daniel had wanted to go back to their home in North Palm Beach since the day after the catastrophic hurricane ripped across south Florida. He was convinced that things would soon return to normal and that they could all resume life as they knew it before, despite the fact that rioting and anarchy had begun long before the storm arrived. It took Eric's arrival with a firsthand report of the conditions there to convince Daniel that going back to his old neighborhood wasn't an option. Even with that information, he wasn't ready to give up Florida entirely. He'd been miserable during their stay in Bart's isolated riverside bungalow, but nevertheless, would have preferred that they all stay there rather than leave the state on a sailboat.

Bart wouldn't have minded if Daniel *had* stayed behind, and in fact would have gladly given him his house that he had no more use for just to be rid of him and his complaining. But Daniel had a son who needed his father, no matter how incompetent, and leaving the two of them there alone was unfair to the boy. Daniel couldn't protect him, and staying would surely amount to a death sentence for both sooner or later. Shauna was too close to Andrew to even hear of it, and besides, Andrew wanted to leave on the boat as much as the rest of them. In the end, Daniel was simply outnumbered and outvoted, and had finally relented and agreed to do the sensible thing and go with them. That didn't mean he'd agreed not to complain though, and Bart knew it was going to get old fast. He or Eric would end up putting a stop to it, of that Bart had no doubt; he just wasn't ready to deal with it now. He had more pressing things on his mind at the moment, mainly the prospect of a nearly 500-mile voyage across the Gulf of Mexico.

The 42-foot schooner was as ready for sea as she could be given the time frame Bart had to work with, and he wasn't particularly worried about the crossing from a seaworthiness standpoint. The Canadian couple that had owned her since she was built and launched as *Tropicbird* had been quite meticulous about staying on top of the maintenance, and over the years the pros working in Bart's yard had completed the tasks they couldn't handle themselves. In addition, because the owners used the Colvin-designed schooner as it was intended, for long cruises among the islands of the Bahamas and other nearby tropical escapes, the vessel was well equipped for sustained periods off-grid in remote anchorages.

The 50-horse Perkins auxiliary diesel was as reliable as a stone axe and the tools and spares to maintain it were already on board. With both of the built-in fuel tanks full and another 60 gallons of fuel in jerry cans lashed to the decks, they had enough diesel to motor all the way across to the Louisiana coast and back if need be. That they would need to was highly unlikely though. Even this time of year there would be enough wind to sail once they reached open water, and the schooner-rigged Colvin Gazelle had the capacity to fly plenty of canvas to take advantage of light breezes.

Once Bart had made the decision to take the vessel, knowing full well that her elderly owners would never return to south Florida, he had set to work creating checklists of tasks to be done and stores to load. Eric and Jonathan did most of the heavy work, but Shauna and Andrew certainly did their part too, and even Daniel made a half-hearted attempt to appear helpful. The bottom was repainted and the wooden spars got three fresh coats of varnish before they were remounted in the tabernacles that would enable the crew to step them without a crane. Both masts were standing and fully rigged now, as all the remaining bridges between them and the Gulf had a minimum 55-foot vertical clearance, giving them room to spare. The relatively low rig was one of the things Bart liked so much about the gaff-rigged schooner. It had been designed and built here on this very river with those clearances in mind.

Between what he already had stored in his house and what they rounded up from among all the vessels stored in his boatyard, Bart compiled enough non-perishable foods to last the six of them four to six months. What they would do when that ran out, he wasn't sure, but in the world they found themselves in now, six months was so far out it was hardly worth considering. For now, the only goal was getting across the Gulf so they could ascend the Atchafalaya River and get to his younger son's place if possible. From there, Eric would find a way to continue overland to Colorado, but that was something he would work out after getting more intel on the overall situation from Keith.

The passage to Louisiana was doable in a matter of days in ideal conditions, but Bart knew anything could happen along the way to delay them, and he'd warned the others to figure on a week or more. None of them had any idea what they might find when they reached the northern Gulf coast, and they could only hope that the river would still be navigable in the aftermath of the hurricane that had struck there after leaving Florida in ruins.

Regardless of any storm damage, Bart already knew that Keith had been dealing with the insurrection that had swept the nation. Despite his rural south Louisiana location, he'd inevitably been drawn into it as a deputy sheriff in a jurisdiction within easy reach of Baton Rouge. It had been several weeks since Bart's last conversation with him via ham radio, and until they got there, it would be impossible to know whether Keith and his wife Lynn were still there or even alive. Bart knew Keith would do everything within reason to fulfill his duties as a sworn law enforcement officer, but in the current conditions, survival and taking care of his family would eventually take priority. Living where they did, Bart figured the two of them might be as well off as anyone could be, at least if his youngest boy didn't throw away his life in some misguided attempt to save a hopeless city.

Bart certainly wasn't planning to get involved in the fighting, but he was as ready as he could reasonably be to respond to the threats he knew they were bound to face. He'd had a small collection of choice rifles and handguns since long before the country began unraveling. Raised in rural Arkansas in a time when most everyone still hunted, Bart had been a crack shot with his .22 a decade before he was old enough to join the Marines and ship off with his unit to southeast Asia in 1969 He certainly hadn't craved more war after what he saw in the jungles of Vietnam, but the experience made a permanent imprint on his perceptions of society and civilizations. Bart knew that peace and security was an illusion, and that it could be taken away in short order. Over there, he saw women and children pressed into combat as a matter of survival. He also saw entire villages massacred because the residents were unarmed and defenseless. Bart vowed that he would never let himself be in that situation, and when he returned home he'd kept up his shooting and combat fitness despite decades of civilian life. He'd been right about needing both the skills and the weapons someday, and he'd also been right to pass on as much of that knowledge as he could to his two sons. Both of them had ended up in careers that put those skills to the test quite frequently—especially Eric. If anybody had what it was going to take to cross half a continent in the current conditions and find Megan, it was her father, Eric. And Bart would do whatever it took to help him, no matter what the risk, which they all knew was considerable.

"I'm getting worried about them," Shauna said, when another twenty minutes passed after the sound of the strangers' boat had faded away in the distance. "They should have had time to get there and back by now."

"Yeah, but you know they probably had some talking to do. I don't think it's been long enough to worry just yet."

Bart wouldn't admit it to Shauna, but of course he was worried too. There was no way of knowing what Eric and Jonathan would encounter at that river blockade. They could be simply turned away, or they could be detained or shot on sight. It was a risk the two of them were well aware of before they left, and one they had discussed at length with Bart while all this was in the planning stages. The meeting with whoever was in charge of that blockade could go either way, and when Eric and Jonathan left the schooner to go on ahead in the skiff, Bart knew it might be the last time he ever saw either of them. The question they'd all had to consider beforehand was the 'what if?' and 'what next?' if for whatever reason they *didn't* come back. They had discussed this beforehand too, and Eric had made Bart promise he wouldn't come looking for them if they weren't back in a reasonable amount of time. Eric assured him that if they couldn't return on their own, there was probably nothing anyone could do to help them. Jonathan's participation in all this was strictly voluntary of course, but the kid had insisted on going along to help after Shauna suggested it might help Eric's case.

"If they think he's your son, that'll be more convincing than just some lone stranger telling them he's seeking passage through the blockade for his family," she'd said.

"Maybe, but he needs a haircut if he's going to pass for any son of mine!"

26

Jonathan balked at that idea, but he'd already agreed to go and help Eric, so he consented to letting Bart give him a military buzz with his clippers before they'd left the bungalow.

"That's a lot better," Eric had said, as Jonathan sat there feeling his newly peeled head. "You wanna learn how to do this commando stuff, the first step is to look like one!" Eric said.

"A lot of those Special Forces dudes I've seen on TV let their hair grow out. And look at that freakin' thick beard you've got!" Jonathan grumbled. His own beard was too thin and patchy to ever fill out like Eric's.

Shauna assured him that he looked much more manly and sexy with his new hairstyle, and beaming at her compliment, Jonathan stopped his complaining. Before the two of them left, Bart had agreed to Eric's conditions and had promised he would turn back and do what he could to look after Shauna and her family if it came to that. Maybe they could make their way to the Atlantic coast through the waterway going east or maybe they couldn't, but if Eric and Jonathan failed to return, they would know leaving by way of the Gulf wasn't an option. Every minute that passed gave Bart more time to ponder what he would actually do in that worst-case scenario. It would be hard, turning away and not knowing what had become of his eldest son when he had arrived here just days ago and Bart didn't want to think about it. When

Andrew suddenly pointed downriver and shouted that they were coming, Bart was relieved to no longer have to. Eric and Jonathan were both in the skiff, speeding around the last bend to where *Dreamtime* was waiting.

Bart put down his rifle and stood at the rail as he watched them approach. Eric and Jonathan had returned unharmed, but had they accomplished what they set out to do? Soon, he would know.

Three

"I DIDN'T PUSH THEM with any unnecessary questions," Eric said, as the rest of the crew gathered around when he and Jonathan were back on board, "but it appears that the men running the blockade are just local citizens. Some of them were obviously commercial fishermen before; their boats are anchored just inside the line of barges. I don't think we have to worry about being searched or arrested, but they do want to see proof that we didn't steal the boat."

"So there goes the whole plan, right out the window," Daniel said, "because the boat *is* stolen. You don't know that some of those men aren't former police officers just because they aren't in uniform. If they look closely enough, the fake papers and changed name aren't going to fool them. Then we will all be arrested or shot. It sounds too risky to me."

Eric ignored Daniel's comments and continued with what he had to say to Bart and Shauna. "As long as they believe we're not looters or boat thieves, I don't think they could care less where we're going or why, or what we have on board.

They *do* want a rather exorbitant price to let us through though."

"Figures," Bart said. "Maybe you shouldn't have shown them any gold after all," Bart said. "We probably could have traded a couple of rifles and pistols instead."

"Probably, but it's too late for that now. I left the half-Krugerrand for a deposit. The man agreed to take the skiff and outboard in exchange for it when we get there. If you'd rather not, I'll give him the gold. It's up to you, Dad. It's your boat."

"I reckon that's just as well with me. That motor alone is worth a lot more than the time it'll take those fellows to move a barge, but I guess it's their gate and they're the gatekeepers, so they get to name their price. We'd probably have to cut the skiff loose out there in the Gulf anyway."

Eric knew his father would prefer to keep the little runabout if it were feasible. They had agreed to tow it behind *Dreamtime* as long as the conditions allowed, and there was a chance they could get it all the way to Louisiana on a long towline if the seas were smooth enough not to swamp it or slam it into the hull of the schooner. Of course they would have to cut it loose at the first sign of trouble and Bart knew that as well as Eric, so giving it up now to get through that river blockade was a reasonable alternative to paying with a coin that would surely come in handy later. Besides, they had an inflatable Zodiac dinghy lashed to the coach roof of the schooner, along with a 15-horse Yamaha outboard to power it. Eric's Klepper kayak that he'd used to approach the coast from offshore was also on board, lashed to the stanchions on the port rail forward. Between it and the dinghy they had the means to abandon ship in an emergency and to ferry the crew to and from shore when they made landfall.

"I imagine Keith can hook you up with another skiff once we reach the Atchafalaya."

"I'm sure he can, son. We'll worry about that when we get there. I'm just glad those men agreed to let us out without a fight."

"You and me both, Dad. But we're not out yet. I'll breathe easier when we drop Florida under the horizon."

Shauna agreed that the trade sounded reasonable, much to the dismay of her husband, who still was far from convinced.

"How do you know this isn't a trap?" he asked Eric. "You and Jonathan told those men you had this big sailboat waiting upriver with your family aboard, and that you wanted out so we could leave on a long voyage. That tells them right there that the boat must be loaded with supplies and other useful stuff. If they have dishonest intentions, then of course they would tell you to come on down there. It just makes things that much easier for them."

"When did you decide folks couldn't be trusted?" Bart asked him. "The whole time you've been here you've doubted

31

what I've been telling you about how dangerous it is to travel, and doubted me when I said the law wasn't going to be able to do anything about it."

"I understand now that it's worse than I originally thought, but I was talking about Palm Beach County, not here. I don't know anything about this part of Florida, but this whole blockade thing sounds suspicious to me."

"Of course it's suspicious," Eric said. "And you're absolutely right. It could be a trap and they could kill us all and take the boat and all our stuff. There's only one way to find out if that's going to happen or if they're going to let us through like they said they would."

"But why? We could still turn back and try to follow the waterway out to the east coast. I know it's farther, and there might be a blockade or ambush somewhere that way too, but we *know* there's one this way."

"Yep, we know what we're dealing with here, and at least they were willing to talk and make a deal. I'll take that as a good sign. A long delay might send the wrong message though. I say we get going and get this over with. Is everyone else in agreement?"

They all nodded except Andrew, who just looked down, staring at the deck beneath his feet, unwilling to vote against his father but also unwilling to side with him and defend his position. Eric already knew the boy wanted to leave. He much preferred the prospect of going to sea on the schooner to staying any longer in Bart's isolated little bungalow where there was nothing to do and little to look forward to.

"It's going to be fine, Andrew. Why don't you come with me up to the bow and help me haul the anchor?"

The boy followed him to the windlass, and Eric let him have a turn at cranking the handle as Bart eased the schooner forward under power to ease the tension on the rode. The sails were bent on and the running rigging organized, but they would stay furled for now. There wouldn't be any sailing until they were clear of the blockade and clear of the shallow waters near Sanibel Island, but Eric and Bart wanted to be ready before they left the river. Once they were beyond the blockade, the last thing they wanted to have to do was sort out all that.

Eric knew Daniel could be right about running into a trap, of course. There was always a chance they could be betrayed by those men guarding the river mouth, but still, Eric didn't think it was likely. After his meeting with them, he leaned towards his original assumption that they were simply local fishermen and other citizens who'd banded together for security purposes. Being boatmen, they'd recognized the importance of restricting access to the Caloosahatchee early on, and having the means to do so with plenty of industrial barges conveniently nearby, they had taken the matter into their own hands. Eric was sure that many communities around the nation would be doing the same in one form or another—at least those places that still had a surviving population of willing and able-bodied men. The choice was simple in the absence of law and order—either band together and fight back or let those willing to take what they wanted by force have their way. Because he understood this, Eric didn't mind paying the price these men demanded, whether it seemed reasonable or not.

Nevertheless, once the anchors were up and the boat was moving downriver with Bart at the helm, Eric went to work making preparations for the worst. He would be the one going ahead alone to deliver the skiff once the schooner was within sight of the barricade, as he'd been the one doing the negotiations. Like before, he would carry only his concealed Glock for defense, and he wanted everyone else to appear unarmed as well, like the family seeking safety he'd portrayed them to be. The weapons would be out of sight, but Eric distributed several loaded rifles around the decks, including his two personal M4's, tucking them beneath the dinghy, seat cushions and other hideaways within easy reach. If anything happened, Bart, Shauna and Jonathan could grab a weapon from wherever they happened to be on the deck at the time, giving them at least a fighting chance. They would be at a great disadvantage though, and they all knew it, so it was strictly a last resort. The men at the blockade outnumbered them and would be watching them closely with weapons already in hand from higher, protected positions aboard the steel barges.

Bart kept to the middle of the channel to stay as far as possible from the banks that were increasingly urban with every mile. They passed storm-damaged and burned out homes and businesses, and cleared the final bridge spans with just inches to spare above the VHF radio antenna at the top of the mainmast. There were a few small powerboats out and about on the river at this midmorning hour, but all of them gave the schooner a wide berth when passing, including a center-console fishing boat that Bart pointed out, telling Eric it had approached them while he and Jonathan were away. When they rounded the final bend and came in view of the blockade, it was obvious to Eric there had been some activity since he and Jonathan had left. One of the big steel-hulled fishing boats had upped anchor and was rafted alongside one of the barges, which appeared to have been pulled aside by its anchors until it was perpendicular to the rest. From what he could tell, Eric thought the opening was wide enough for *Dreamtime* to transit. He directed Bart to the spot where the man had told him to have the crew stand-by in the sailboat, and then he climbed over the side into the skiff, carrying with him a Ziploc bag containing the forged ship's papers for *Dreamtime*.

"I suppose I'll hop back on board when you come through the gap. Don't sail off and leave me! I'll call you on

Channel 16 with their instructions as soon as they tell me what they want you to do. Keep your eyes and ears open and wish me luck!"

Eric motored away with Shauna calling after him to be careful. It sounded sincere, whether because she still cared about him or because she knew that without him there would be no finding their daughter, Megan. Daniel, on the other hand, was so nervous he could barely speak, and was now pacing the deck, certain that what they were doing was a mistake. But when Eric pulled up to the opening formed by the relocated barge, the man he'd spoken with before was there to greet him. It appeared he was a man of his word, and Eric tossed him a line as he shut off the outboard and let the skiff drift alongside.

"Looks like that was easy enough," Eric said, nodding at the opening that was clearly sufficient for the schooner to exit."

"Not as easy as you might think. In fact it was more trouble than we figured, moving three anchors and then having to reset them with the tide falling like it is. It'll be even harder to put back after you're gone."

"But you'll have a nice little skiff and great Yamaha outboard for your trouble. Have you got my coin?"

"I do, and that's what I'm saying. It was more trouble than we thought, so we had to raise the price. The boat and outboard, plus the coin will cover it, but I'm going to need to see your ship's paperwork... proof of ownership like we discussed. I suppose that's what you've got in the bag there, but we're going to need to come aboard and inspect the vessel too... make sure you're not carrying stolen goods. Unless of course you happen to have found another one of those coins. Then we can waive all those formalities and just let you sail right through."

"That's not what we agreed on," Eric said, fighting to suppress the rage building inside him at the man's treachery and greed. "That's more than double, in fact! I thought we had a deal!"

"It was more like an estimate, if you want to look at it that way. If your father owned a boatyard, then you should know how that works. Somebody brings in a vessel for maintenance and repairs, and it turns out there's almost always more work to be done than it seemed at first glance; extra labor and extra parts and materials, just like at the auto repair shop. That's why there are always two prices in such establishments: an estimate and then a final invoice. That's just the nature of the business. Surely you understand?"

Eric knew by the finality of the man's tone that further negotiation was off the table. The choice was to either agree to his terms, or turn back and figure out another way to get *Dreamtime* out to sea. He wasn't prepared to spend weeks attempting to go east through the waterway and around the peninsula of Florida to get to the Gulf when it was right there in sight beyond that gap. There were nearly a dozen men armed with rifles watching and waiting for his answer, so he made the decision without hesitation.

"Fine. I'll go back and get the other coin, but it's staying in my pocket until our boat is outside this barricade."

"Good decision! When you get over there, tell your father or whoever is at the helm to keep it nice and slow, well under five knots, and to steer right for the center of the gap. Tell him not to stop until he is completely outside of the river mouth and in the channel out there. You come back here in the skiff first though and bring the other coin with you. Once you've paid up, one of my guys will run you back to your boat when it's out there in the clear.

"Oh, and one other thing: I know you're probably carrying weapons on board. If you're not, then you ought to be. When you get back over there, make sure to tell your crew that if we see one of them brandishing a firearm of any kind, the men will open fire without hesitation."

Eric nodded but said nothing. He wasn't going to acknowledge the weapons even though he was paying to avoid a vessel search. The sooner he could get this over with and leave this place behind, the better, because if anything else came up, these men would probably want even more to let them through. Bart wasn't going to like it, but the gold was Eric's and if it took every bit of it to make his way to wherever Megan was, then so be it. He sped back to the schooner and climbed aboard with the news, and then disappeared below to retrieve the coin from his stash.

"This is exactly what I told you was going to happen," Daniel said. "Now that they know you have gold, and that you're paying them not to come aboard and look around, they're just going to assume we're loaded down with more gold and illicit cargo. They'll probably shoot us all once we get near that opening. This is crazy!"

"You may be right," Eric said, "but it's still our best option. If you want out I'll run you ashore now, before we go through with it. It's up to you." Eric pointed to the small beach on point upstream of the blockade, the same hidden beach from which he and Jonathan had launched the kayak after sneaking across the point that night they began their journey upriver.

"Don't do it, Daniel," Shauna said. "Eric has experience with situations like this. Just trust him and let him handle it."

"That didn't work out so well for you and Megan, did it?"

"Don't even, Daniel! This is a matter of survival now. We're all going to be better off once we're out of Florida."

"Whatever. I'm outvoted five to one anyway," Daniel said, glaring back at her and then at Andrew before entering the companionway to go below. "I don't want to see it when they start shooting. I guess they'll just kill me later when they come aboard for the loot!"

Eric grinned at the look of disgust on Shauna's face. Whatever she saw in this guy when she married him wasn't evident now. Poor Andrew didn't know what to do or say. Eric gave him a wink and assured him it was going to be all right. Then he turned to Bart as he climbed back into the skiff. "Let's do this. I'm ready to get it over with!"

Four

ERIC RETURNED TO THE barge where the man he'd been negotiating with was waiting, and showed him the second coin, putting it back in the pocket of his shorts afterwards as they waited for *Dreamtime* to approach the gap. Eric wasn't volunteering information, but now that the man in charge had what he wanted, he seemed genuinely interested in their proposed voyage across the Gulf. Without getting too specific, Eric truthfully told him he had a brother on the northern Gulf coast that they were going to try and get out, and that he didn't know where they'd go from there. He didn't mention his daughter in Colorado, and that he was going there for her too, even if he had to walk.

"We've heard the hurricane damage is even worse up there than it was in Florida. I'm not surprised really, as warm as the Gulf has been this year. The big ones always strengthen when they get out over the Gulf, and the shallow water off the coast up there makes the storm surge a lot worse than here."

"That seems to be the pattern," Eric agreed.

"You're going to see a lot more than storm damage though if you end up near any of the cities up there, especially Houston, New Orleans or Mobile. It was as bad or worse there than it was in Miami or Tampa. I'm sure they had already cut the power grid in most of those places before the hurricane hit. It was a war zone, man."

"I'm sure it was. We don't have any intentions of going to any of those cities. And we don't plan to stay in the area long anyway. Just get in, get my brother and his wife, and get out."

"But get out to where? If you're not part of a community with organized defenses like we have here, you and your family won't last long no matter where you go. It's like this all over the country."

"So we'll *leave* the country then. I never figured on staying here after what's happened anyway."

"Good luck then. If I were you, I'd be on my way out from here. Going up there to look for your brother is probably a lost cause, and it'll probably get you all killed. But that's a decision you'll have to make."

Eric nodded and turned his attention back to the schooner, which was slowly approaching the gap under Bart's guidance. Jonathan was at the bow, ready if Bart needed him to toss a line or put out a fender, while Shauna stood at the back of the main cabin, next to the companionway. He didn't see either Daniel or Andrew. Obviously, they were both below in the cabin. The men surrounding him on the barges were watching closely, but weren't pointing their weapons in the direction of the boat. Five minutes later, the schooner was well past the gap and Bart had cut the power to let it drift in the outside channel. Eric reached in his pocket to retrieve the coin, and once he'd paid up, the man in charge told one of the others to give Eric his promised ride out to the sailboat. Eric showed no emotion as the two of them pulled away from the blockade, but he was feeling better every second. His escort said nothing during the short ride and that was just as well with Eric. If he tried anything at the last minute, Eric would draw the Glock and kill him, but he was soon back aboard *Dreamtime* with no further drama.

"Let's get the hell out of here," he said to Bart.

"It can't be soon enough, son!" Bart pushed the shift lever to forward and slowly brought the diesel up to cruising speed as he pointed the bow south to follow the winding channel that would lead them to the center span of the Sanibel Causeway visible in the distance.

"They don't seem to be in a big hurry to move that barge back, Shauna said, after they were well out of rifle range of the men at the blockade but still within view.

Eric took the binoculars when she handed them to him and saw that she was right. The gap was still open, and there was activity among the anchored fleet of fishing vessels. "Maybe they're just rearranging things since they had to reset anchors and move the barge anyway. Who knows? I suppose it doesn't matter to us."

He didn't think much more of it until they were well past the bridge overpass and making their way southwest in the channel leading to the Gulf beyond Sanibel Island. Daniel had finally come back on deck, and Eric pointed out that they were all still alive and unharmed.

"Maybe so, but why are those boats following us?"

Eric turned to look back where he was pointing. Sure enough, two of the big shrimp trawlers were outside the blockade and in the outbound channel, but that didn't necessarily mean they were following the schooner.

"Just relax man. It looks like they're going fishing. They probably decided that since they've already gone to the trouble to move that barge, they ought to send a couple boats out to make a few runs with the nets. If they wanted to rob us or hurt us, they would have done it when we were right there in reach and they could have easily prevented us from leaving at all."

"It just seems suspicious to me. They're definitely coming this way."

"That's because there's only one channel out to the Gulf from there. They have to come the same way we did to reach open water. They'll turn off and go about their business soon. You'll see. Besides, they're at least a mile behind us now."

"We'll keep an eye on them to be sure," Bart said, "but once we get past the south end of the island and make our turn to the northwest, I expect you'll see them heading somewhere else."

"Hey Jonathan!" Eric shouted. "Let's get ready to hoist some sail! Soon as we make the turn past the island there ought to be enough breeze."

"Absolutely dude, just tell me what to do!"

"It's not a lot different than the little Catalina we sailed over here. Just a few more strings to pull and an extra mast. You'll have to put your back into those halyards though. Everything is bigger."

"I figured that. I got it though!"

Shauna jumped in to help and after several minutes of hard work hauling and cleating halyards and adjusting sheets, the main, fore and main staysails were up. Bart still hadn't slacked off the throttle on the engine though. The breeze was light this early in the day, especially since it was out of the east and the land was still close and to windward.

"We should set the jib and forestaysail too as soon as we make our northward turn," Bart said. "We may have to motorsail for a while, but I'll bet in another hour we can shut down the diesel."

"I say we run it anyway unless the wind picks up enough that we can sail at full hull speed without it," Eric said.

"Fuel's not an issue, and we're not out here to enjoy the serenity."

"That's fine with me. Getting to Keith's is all that matters. If we need more fuel later, he'll probably have a good idea where we can get some. With all of the refineries on that coast, if there's any available anywhere, it'll be somewhere up there."

Eric knew those issues were too far out in the future to think about now. Getting to Megan in Colorado and then getting her back to the boat would take some doing. *One step at a time...* he kept reminding himself. *One step at a time....*

"Those guys are still behind us," Jonathan said.

Eric already knew it, of course, because he'd been keeping an eye on them all along, despite all the other tasks associated with getting the sails set and trimmed. There was still no reason to doubt that the fishing boats had left the river to go to work. The only thing odd about it was that they were still hanging so far back, matching *Dreamtime's* pace from more than a half-mile astern. By now, they could have opened up their engines to get wherever they were going at twelve knots or better, but for some reason, they were holding half that, running the speed of the much slower sailboat. It wasn't because they didn't have room to pass either; the channel was plenty wide enough at this point.

"They're probably just running at half throttle to conserve fuel," Eric said. "It makes sense to do so if you're thinking long term these days."

Daniel, of course, wasn't convinced. "Following us until we get far enough offshore is more likely. That way, there won't be any witnesses."

"Do you think they are going to kill us, Dad?" Andrew asked.

"No, of course they're not, Andrew!" Shauna said, glaring at Daniel as she did so. "Your dad is just being paranoid. Eric paid those men the price they wanted to let us out. They're not going to bother us now."

"She's right," Eric said. "If anything, maybe they're just messing with us. It must be boring sitting there at that blockade all day with nothing to do. This could be a little game for them."

Two hours later, however, they still had company and Eric wasn't so sure that Daniel's fears weren't justified. *Dreamtime* was now far enough out in the Gulf that the mainland of Florida was just a sliver of blue-green on the distant horizon, with only a few of the tallest buildings standing out from the hazy outline of the coast. They were sailing well now, reaching to the north in a 12 to 15 knot breeze that was enough to move the schooner along at eight knots with minimal assist from the engine. Out here there was just enough of a sea running to give her a lively motion, and Daniel soon felt queasy and went below to lie down, despite Bart's warning that being in the cabin would probably make it worse. Eric hoped he stayed there for now though, as he didn't need Daniel's panic affecting the rest of the crew if it turned out he was right to mistrust the fishermen.

Their intentions became more suspect with every mile now, as the two trawlers mirrored the relatively slow pace of the schooner, following in their wake from the same distance astern. The only thing that had changed was that they had spread out from single file and were now running abeam of each other about a quarter-mile apart. It wasn't looking good, as it appeared to Eric that they might indeed be planning and positioning for an attack. But if that were the case, what were they waiting for? Was it as Daniel suggested? Were they waiting until the schooner was completely out of sight of land so they could be sure there were no witnesses? If so, it seemed hardly necessary, as they hadn't passed any other boats once they were outside of the channel entrance near Sanibel Island, and obviously no one was around to see anything that might happen.

A pod of dolphins that suddenly showed up to take turns playing in the bow wave gave Eric the opportunity to quietly discuss the situation with Bart. Jonathan had spotted them first, and when he yelled to Andrew and pointed them out, the two of them rushed up there to get a closer look, followed by Shauna. Eric stayed next to Bart by the helm, studying the two boats through his binoculars.

"I thought about calling them on the VHF to ask them what in the hell they're doing, but decided against it," Bart said. "If they *are* up to no good, they probably won't answer anyway."

"Probably not. The longer they stay back there, the more likely I think it is they're up to something. I'm going below to get my gear ready. If they come at us from two angles, like it appears they might, we can't afford to let them make the first move."

"No, and we sure can't outrun them," Bart agreed. "We'll have to take it to them and hit 'em before they realize we're willing and able. It's the only advantage we've got. I'm not sure how much longer they're gonna wait, unless they're holding out for dark."

"If they *do* wait that long, it could work in our favor, but I'm not counting on it," Eric said. "Best to be ready now."

When Eric went below, Daniel was just emerging from the head compartment, looking pale and unsteady. He'd obviously gone in there to throw up, and he looked to Eric like he wasn't finished."

"Feeling any better yet?"

"No. I don't know why I would get seasick in these conditions. I've been deep sea fishing in much worse."

"Every boat's got a different motion. Some may affect you while others don't. It could be something you ate too, or the stress we're all dealing with. You'll get used to it and get over it soon, I'm sure."

"Are those two boats still back there?"

"Yep. I'm afraid so."

"So they *are* going to attack us, aren't they? We're not anywhere near a channel now. You can't tell me they're still on the way to some fishing grounds. So what are we going to do?"

"We'll do what we're doing now; maintain course and keep a close eye on them. I'm getting prepared now. If they try something, we'll hit them with everything we've got before they hit us."

"I knew it! I knew it was going to come to this!"

"If it does, we'll handle it. They could have done it at the blockade where we'd have been severely outnumbered and unable to move. Or they could have come upriver and hit us at the boatyard or the house before we even left. It's no more dangerous to be out here than anywhere else we might be."

"My son doesn't deserve to die like this. He's only twelve! Maybe we can negotiate with them. Have you tried to call them on the radio? They probably think you have more of those gold coins. You probably do, don't you? You're going to have to give them to them. They won't have any reason to kill us if you give them what they want."

"If they wanted to demand more than I gave them, they would have done it at the blockade. They would have searched the boat then and there and never let us out. It's pretty clear to me they must have talked it over after we were already out and decided to come after whatever else we might have."

"So give it to them then! Better that than to die!"

"What if it's not just the gold they want, Daniel? What if they want the boat too? If so, they're not going to want us on board in their way. They'll kill us all and dump us over the side for the sharks. Or what if they say they want Shauna? What then, Daniel? She's *your* wife now. Should we just give her to them?"

Daniel looked sicker than ever as he realized he didn't have the answers. Eric turned his attention to the gear piled in his bunk. He pulled out his largest dry bag and opened it up, checking the rifle with the mounted grenade launcher and gathering all the hi-explosive rounds he had for it in two bandoliers so he could reload in a hurry. Then he double-checked his rifle mags to make sure they were all topped off. Both of his M4's were chambered for 5.56, but they had Bart's full collection of firearms to choose from as well. Bart had his favorite, the .308 caliber Springfield M1-A already close at hand in the cockpit. There was a Mossberg shotgun and a semi-automatic SKS in 7.62x39 that he'd taken off the recent looters he'd shot in the boatyard. A similar incident had netted him a decent AK-47 in the same caliber, along with half a dozen 30-round mags for it. Another of Bart's personal favorites was a stainless-steel lever-action .45-70 loaded with 405-grain hard cast bullets. Bart had shown it to Eric when they were first moving all their things aboard the boat. It was short and handy, designed to be easy to carry whether walking or on horseback.

"I bought it three or four years ago, when I started planning that fishing trip to Alaska," Bart had said. "Those hard-cast lead rounds will put down a grizzly. It takes a heavy bullet to penetrate all that bone and muscle, and they oughta to do pretty well on steel too. It'll make a good boat gun; it's short and handy, and being stainless, it won't rust. It'll make bigger holes in a boat hull than anything else we've got, and those rounds should go right through an outboard motor too. Hell, they'll take out a diesel engine block if you can figure out where it is."

Eric had no doubt the levergun would be effective, and he liked the feel of it. Bart also had a couple more 12-gauge shotguns; one that was a sporting type automatic and the other a more compact pump-action riot gun with an extended magazine that held eight rounds. Loaded with buckshot, a 12-gauge was a formidable weapon at close range and shooting slugs would from one of those would make big holes in an attacking boat too.

They certainly had what they needed to repel boarders if another boat got that close, but what Eric really wished for was more firepower to engage an approaching vessel at range. The M203 grenade launcher had proven its worth when he and Jonathan had the encounter off Biscayne Bay, even though the round had harmlessly exploded in the water, but it wasn't exactly a precision weapon when used from a moving boat against a moving target. He was glad to have it and was sure he would be putting it to use, but it would be nice to have a belt-fed M60 or better yet, a deck mounted 50-caliber M2. Eric could have procured those kinds of weapons easily before he left to come back to Florida, but knowing there was only so much he could carry in the kayak during his covert insertion, he'd reluctantly shown some restraint.

Both times he'd approached the river blockade, including that first visit with Jonathan, Eric had scoped out the cluster of fishing boats anchored there without making it obvious. He was looking for just such weaponry, as he knew it was possible that heavier guns would start turning up on civilian vessels. If there were any aboard though, they were covered or disguised, and studying the two trailing boats through the binoculars, he still didn't see anything of the kind. He could only hope they weren't packing superior firepower, because it was bad enough that there were two of them, giving them the option to attack from different sides at once. Eric was running through the possible scenarios in his mind, having already switched to full combat mode, even if he wasn't ready to alarm his entire crew just yet.

"Bart said he was going to teach Andrew and me to shoot," Daniel said sheepishly, as Eric started up the companionway ladder with the extra M4. "He never got around to it though. He said it would make too much noise. You can blame him that we can't do anything to help out now."

"Yeah, I know," Eric said. "It's all his fault. I'll make sure Andrew is down here with you before the shooting starts. Stay as low in the hull as you can, and the two of you should be fine."

Five

"WHAT ARE YOU GOING to do?" Shauna asked, when she saw Eric climbing back into the cockpit with all the weapons he'd hauled up from below. She had just returned aft from the bow, where Jonathan and Andrew were still lying on the foredeck, trying to reach down and touch one of the broaching dolphins. Eric was already studying the two boats again through his binoculars, but he knew the sight of the M4 with the grenade launcher and bandoliers of grenades beside it had gotten his ex-wife's attention, as he hadn't mentioned to her previously that he had them on board.

"I'm going to keep watching them and keep alert. What else?"

"You said earlier that you didn't think they were following us. They are though, aren't they?"

"Yes, I'm afraid so."

"What do you think they're waiting for then? If they're going to try something, why wait?"

"I guess they figure time is on their side, so they're not in a hurry. Maybe they're waiting for night, because they'd rather attack in the dark. Who knows? But they're coming, you can bet on that."

"Don't you think you should call them on the radio? You could warn them that we're armed and that we'll shoot if they come any closer."

"It won't do any good. They probably already assume we're armed, just not as well as we really are. I don't want them to know we're concerned about their presence. The radio is on now just as it's been ever since we left this morning. If they try to call us and order us to stop or something, we'll hear it, but I'm not calling them first."

"I think we should change course," Bart said. "We can fall off about thirty degrees to the west-southwest for a while and it won't make any difference in the long run. We can correct it later. A course change will tell us for sure that they're going to try something, and if we're on that heading they'll have the sun right in their eyes when it gets lower on the horizon. They won't be able to see the details of what we're doing then, even with binoculars."

"That's good thinking, Dad. It won't be long before it's at a low enough angle to blind them. We can certainly use that to our advantage." Eric had already thought of this when he went below to get the weapons. There was no harm in letting Bart take credit for the idea though. His father was an old soldier with combat experience of his own, and he'd taught

Eric a lot long before he was old enough to enlist and get his own first taste of battle.

"You're not going to shoot first are you?" Shauna asked. "What if we're wrong about their intentions?"

"If they close the gap enough to be in rifle range, their intentions will be pretty obvious. I don't plan on letting them open up on us from two directions at once. We're already at a disadvantage, outnumbered and exposed out here in the open like this on a much slower vessel."

"This entire boat is made of metal. Will it stop bullets?"

"Most parts of it probably won't," Bart said. "The hull skin is a tough aluminum alloy, but it's not very thick, at least not above the waterline. Steel-jacketed bullets from a high-powered rifle will go through it with no problem. If you were down below with several bulkheads between you and whoever is firing, you might be okay, but that depends on the weapon. They may not see you down there, but they could still hit you."

"So what you're saying is that going below will offer *concealment*, but not *cover*."

"Exactly! I guess Eric must have taught you the difference."

"A long time ago," Eric said. "But that's exactly right Shauna. No place out here is safe and that's why we can't afford to wait and find ourselves on the defensive. Their boats are steel, and will probably give their crews better protection, but they've got those big windows in their pilothouses. If we hit them hard where they're vulnerable and let them know we're serious about it, they may decide whatever we have on board is not worth the cost. We don't know what *they've* got, but chances are it's just ordinary rifles."

"How close are you going to let them get before you decide that it's too close?" Shauna asked.

"No closer than the effective range of our rifles. And I'd like to hit them with a couple of 203's before I even start shooting. I seriously doubt they'll be expecting anything like that. If we can get in their blind spot with the sun in their eyes, I can get set up to fire the launcher before they realize what's happening."

"Well, you can count on me to do my part, I hope you know that. Just give me a rifle. I don't plan on hiding down below. I was just asking. Andrew certainly needs to stay down there though."

"Yeah, he can keep his Daddy company," Eric said with a smirk, knowing it would get a rise out of Shauna.

"Just drop it, Eric! There's a lot about Daniel you don't know."

"Sorry, it's just that I haven't been around guys like that in a while. Anyway, yes. I want you on a rifle. My other M4 would be best. You're familiar with the AR-15s we used to shoot. That one is essentially the same thing, with the addition of the 3-round burst mode, which will come in handy. Jonathan can take the AK. Dad will have a little more reach and penetration with his .308. If they get close enough, we've got his bear gun to ventilate their hulls." Eric saw Bart smile at the sight of his .45-70 in Eric's bag.

"I'd love the chance to try it out, son, but I think we'd all be better off if we don't let 'em get that close. If you can put a 203 into one of their pilothouses, you're a better man than me, though. I never could hit worth a damn with one of those things."

"I may not be able to do it either, but it's worth a try."

Their discussion was interrupted when Jonathan and Andrew returned to the cockpit, Jonathan telling them that the dolphins had disappeared before the two of them noticed all the weapons Eric had laid out.

"Are those men going to start shooting at us?" Andrew asked. "Is that why you've got all those guns out here?"

"It's okay, Andrew," Shauna said. "Eric is just being prepared. Nothing has happened yet and it may not, but it doesn't hurt to be ready, just in case. It'll be best if you go down in the cabin now. You should go see if your father is feeling better and see if he needs something to drink. He was really seasick earlier." Andrew did as he was asked, but not before staring for a long moment at the two fishing boats.

"When this is over, it's going to be time to teach that boy how to shoot," Eric said.

"I can help," Jonathan said. "Andrew is a pretty cool kid. I think he'll be a fast learner. He wants a chance to try. He's been telling me every day."

"He'll get his chance, but not here and not now. I want him to stay below like Shauna said. Have you ever shot an AK-47 Jonathan? It's not all that different than the M4, just different controls and magazines."

"No, dude, but I've always wanted to. Is it the real deal?"

"No, it's semi-auto, if that's what you mean, but that's okay. You've got six 30-round mags. It's not as accurate as the M4, but we're not going for precision here anyway. It's a bigger and heavier bullet and may penetrate their cabins a little better than the 5.56. The main objective is to lay down steady fire to keep them on the defensive. I plan to start with the grenades. Shauna will dump three or four mags worth of bursts from the other M4 and my father will pick off any targets he can see with his Springfield."

"Dude, that sounds like a solid plan! That one grenade you shot at the boat down south of Miami sure changed their minds. Maybe they will scare these assholes the same way!"

"Maybe, but I'm not trying to scare them. If they come close enough to be in range out here on the high seas, then the gloves come off and they're fair game as far as I'm concerned. We're on our own out here. If we don't stop them, you can bet they won't give us any quarter if they board this vessel."

When Bart changed course, putting them on a new west-southwest heading, the two boats trailing them turned to follow, just as Eric expected they would. They still hadn't broken radio silence on any of the VHF channels he could pick up, but that didn't mean they weren't in communication with each other, probably via walkie talkies or some other type radio in a different frequency band. They probably assumed the course change was in reaction to their shadowing of the schooner, and Eric hoped they would think it was because of fear, rather than a strategic plan for counterattack. If they made their move now, it would make little difference, as the sun was still too high. In another hour though, Eric would have the advantage he wanted. The boats were still spread apart, running beam-on-beam, which put them at a slight angle to either side of *Dreamtime's* stern. They were maintaining their speed and distance perfectly, cruising in formation like a pair of predators running down prey, waiting for the right moment to pounce.

Eric got the extra hour he'd hoped for, as apparently the men aboard the fishing boats were waiting for night. Maybe they thought they could close in quickly in the dark, running without lights until they were close enough that they couldn't miss when they started shooting. Eric could see that both vessels had large spotlights on elevated mounts atop their bridge decks. If they lit up the schooner from both sides with blinding light, it would make it difficult to return accurate fire.

The more he thought of that scenario, the more Eric figured that was their plan, and Bart agreed.

"We'll beat 'em at their own game, only we'll be using the sun."

"It's going to work best for the one that's to starboard," Eric said. "The captain of that one is running dead into the sun now. If we make our move in the next half hour, it'll have maximum effect. That other guy to port won't be as blinded, so we need to hit him first."

"I say we cut the power hard without warning," Bart said. "It'll take them a minute to realize we've stopped, and unless they just stop too, they'll be in range real quick. We can put the helm down to starboard and heave-to to steady the motion, and then she ought to lie off with her starboard rail facing the enemy. That'll give us room to spread out to several firing positions."

"I agree. I'm going to work from the top of the coach roof ahead of the foremast. I can brace against the mast to steady the grenade launcher. As soon as you cut the power I'll help you with the sheets before I get in position. You should be able to get her underway again quickly by falling off under power if necessary."

"Where do you want me?" Jonathan asked. "I can go up forward with you and cover for you."

"That'll be good, but stay low on the port side deck, so you'll at least have the cabin sides between you and their guns. Shauna, I want you to stay low in the companionway. You can stand there on the steps just high enough to shoot over the cockpit coamings. If they open up on us, nowhere on board is going to be totally safe. We need to hit them with everything we've got before they get a chance to get off a lot of return fire."

Daniel, seeing Shauna getting into position with the rifle, now made his way to the companionway to try and talk her into taking cover with him and Andrew.

"You need to stay inside with Andrew, Daniel. Both of you need to get down low and stay there until this is over!"

"Well what about you, Shauna? You may know how to shoot, but you have no business in a gunfight! You should come down here with us."

"Don't worry about me! I'll be fine. The more firepower we have the less likely they'll have a chance to shoot back at all."

"If everybody's ready, it's time to do this!" Eric shouted. "Get in your positions. The sun is dropping fast. We'll lose our window of opportunity!"

With that, Eric moved his gear forward to the foremast. Jonathan got into position next to him, crouching on the side deck with the AK and its spare magazines. The two boats were lit up by the low-angle sunlight, making it easy to pick out all the details on their decks. Using the binoculars, Eric could see a man standing on deck near the bow of the port boat, the AR-type rifle slung across his chest clearly visible and leaving no doubt as to what these 'fishermen' were up to. The rest of the crew was either inside the cabin or up on the bridge deck behind the pilothouse windows, which reflected the light, making it impossible to see inside. He couldn't see anyone at all on the starboard boat.

"See that guy on deck there on the boat that's to port?" Eric asked Jonathan. "He's got a rifle. Dad may take him out first, but in case he misses, I want you to focus on taking him out too as soon as I launch the first grenade. I'm aiming at the pilothouse of that boat first, because they don't have the sun in their eyes as much as the crew of the starboard one. They'll be better able to return fire than the others that are blinded."

"So, you're not even going to give them a warning shot into the water, like you did those other guys in the speedboat?"

"No. This is completely different, Jonathan. In that case there was no way to be sure what the men in that boat wanted, because they just came up fast out of nowhere. These guys have followed us for nearly eight hours. I'm not giving them any more time to prepare their attack. Those boats are moving a lot slower too and they're bigger targets. Once they come into range after we stop, I'll have a good chance of making some solid hits with the grenades. Just make sure that guy you can see doesn't make it to cover where he'll have a chance to fire back!"

"I gotcha dude! Don't worry about me. I can do my part. I'll get him before he has time to even think about shooting our way!"

"Don't fire until you hear the first grenade explode, though. When that guy is down, focus on the pilothouse next. Whether the grenade hits it or not, dump a mag through those windows and reload as quickly as you can. I'll be focusing on putting a grenade into the other one and you can back me up on that one too. We want to hurt them as much as possible in the initial attack, to diminish their ability to retaliate."

Eric was as ready as he'd ever be. He'd instructed Shauna to basically do the same thing as Jonathan. With her M4 and Jonathan's AK, along with Bart looking for targets with the .308, the men aboard those boats were going to be on the defensive. Would it be enough to turn them back? There was only one way to find out. He rushed to the cockpit to help Bart handle the sheets so they could heave-to as soon as Bart cut the power.

"I'm ready if you are. Let's do it, Dad!"

Bart pulled the throttle lever back to idle and put the helm over to bring the bow into the wind enough to luff. As soon as the sheets went slack, Eric and Bart worked quickly to haul the fore and main to the centerline, and then Bart put the helm down to leeward and lashed it in place. Eric was back in position at the base of the foremast before the boat even began to settle in. He glanced at the two fishing boats and saw that they were still steaming forward and had not reduced speed. The gap would close fast, and he steadied himself against the mast with the grenade launcher pointing at his first target. *That's it, just keep coming. Just a little more....*

Dreamtime was still rolling in the two to four foot seas, but the motion was slow and predictable now with the headsails aback and the main sheeted to centerline. Eric timed the roll and pulled the trigger when the deck was as near to level as it would get. The high-explosive projectile left the tube at just the right moment, arcing high through its trajectory before plummeting down again and penetrating the glass windows of the pilothouse. The detonation was instantaneous, and the next thing Eric heard was the first reports from Bart's M1-A, followed instantly by Jonathan's AK and Shauna's M4. Eric saw the man on the deck go down, but his focus was on getting a grenade into the second boat. As he adjusted his aim to his new target, he saw several men pouring out of that second pilothouse with weapons. Bart's steady firing dropped at least one, but the survivors were returning fire now, and Eric heard the incoming bullets hitting metal all around him. He was about to send his second grenade on its way at the peak of the roll when he was distracted by a sharp cry from

Shauna, who suddenly dropped her weapon and disappeared down the companionway steps.

Eric knew she'd been hit, but there was no time to check her status until they could suppress the incoming fire. He aimed the launcher again and let the grenade fly. His timing with the waves wasn't as perfect as the first, and the round missed the pilothouse but exploded on the side deck nearby. Eric saw two more of the men fall, but whether from shrapnel or his companions' rifle fire, he couldn't tell. He flipped the selector switch of the weapon to full auto and unleashed a sustained burst, cutting down at least one more as the others dove for cover. As he dropped the empty mag and inserted another, he swept his sights back to the first boat. It was still running at the same speed, but no one seemed to be in control as it veered off at an angle to the south. Someone was apparently still at the helm of the second one, however. Eric readied another grenade as it slowed and began turning to starboard.

"Go see about Shauna, Jonathan! Use pressure to stop whatever bleeding you see. I'll be right there as soon as I take care of this!"

Six

ERIC PUT HIS NEXT grenade squarely into the port side of the second boat's pilothouse, and when Bart finally stopped shooting, all incoming fire had ceased. Eric scanned both vessels through the binoculars, looking for signs of life, but when he saw nothing moving, he crawled aft to the cockpit where Bart was still kneeling by the helm.

"How bad was Shauna hit, Dad? Did you see?"

"No! I heard her cry out and just saw her stumble back down the ladder after she dropped her weapon. Jonathan says she's bleeding a lot."

"I'm going down there. I'll send him back up to help you with the sheets. We need to fall off and get underway! If any of them are still alive, I don't think they'll follow us after getting hit like that, but I still want to create distance."

Eric was confident that they'd taken out most, if not all of the crew of the two boats. He'd had better success than he'd hoped for with the 203s. Hitting both pilothouses from that distance was as much luck as anything else. Anyone inside those enclosed spaces was likely either dead or badly wounded, and the shrapnel would have damaged equipment and systems. The surprise counterattack had worked brilliantly, and the incoming fire had been minimal considering how outnumbered they were. It was enough to hit Shauna though, and Eric was anxious to find out just how badly she was hurt.

The handrail beside the companionway ladder was slippery with blood as Eric descended into the main salon. Shauna was stretched out on the teak sole with Jonathan and Daniel hovering over her. Andrew, who was sitting on the bunk beside them looked up at him as he entered, his eyes filled with fear and worry for his stepmom. Jonathan was applying pressure with a blood-soaked towel held against her right upper arm while Daniel and had her right hand in both of his, a bloody T-shirt wound tightly around it from her wrist to her fingers.

"Where is she hit?" Eric asked.

"It looks like a bullet went all the way through her arm just below the shoulder," Jonathan said. "One went through her hand too. It's bleeding like crazy!"

"Just keep the pressure on it! I've got something in my kit that should stop the bleeding!"

Eric yanked another of his dry bags open and pulled out his first-aid supplies. He felt like an idiot now for not having this stuff out and ready before the action began, but he'd been so focused on his weapons and strategy that it had slipped his mind. He opened a package of hemostatic combat dressings with a built-in clotting agent and grabbed a Rapid Application Tourniquet in case the hand wound involved an artery.

"I've got this, Jonathan! Go help my dad with the sails so we can get moving ASAP. Check with the binoculars to make sure you don't see anyone still moving aboard those boats, and shoot any you do!"

Eric slid into place next to Shauna and kept the pressure Jonathan had been holding on the towel. Shauna was aware that he was there, and was holding herself together and remaining calm considering how much pain she appeared to be in.

"We stopped them, Shauna. I don't think we have to worry about more trouble from those guys. Taking care of you is the top priority now." Eric turned to Daniel: "How bad is her hand?"

"I don't know, but it looks bad! There was so much blood I couldn't see much of anything. I just wrapped it up to try and stop the bleeding."

"It hurts," Shauna mumbled. "It hurts a lot worse than my shoulder!"

Eric glanced at her rifle where it fell near the base of the steps. The bullet had also shattered the plastic pistol grip she'd been holding. Eric figured the round that hit her must have first struck her trigger hand and the grip and then gone through her upper arm. A couple more inches to the left and it would have been a whole different outcome. When he removed the towel Jonathan had been holding, and saw the entry and exit wounds, Eric felt much better about the situation. The kid had been right about the bullet going all the way through, but even so, it could have fragmented or shattered the bone. At the very least it must have tumbled by the time it tore through the arm, cutting through muscle tissue and doing plenty of damage. The first priority was to stop the blood loss, and after his quick assessment, Eric was confident the clotting agent in the dressings would take care of that.

"Keep the pressure on her hand," Eric told Daniel. "I'm going to patch up her shoulder first. It looks like the round went all the way through, and that's a really good thing."

When he looked at her hand next after removing the bloody shirt, Eric saw that the bullet had ripped through the palm of her hand and out near the back of the wrist before continuing on to her upper arm cutting through the middle metacarpal and likely destroying both nerve and bone. She'd lost plenty of blood, but was lucky that it had apparently missed the larger arteries. Considering the conditions they were in now, without access to surgery, Eric thought she might lose use of the hand, at least partially. Even so, it could have been far worse.

"You're going to have some pain to deal with, Shauna, but nothing life-threatening as long as it doesn't get infected, so you're pretty lucky."

"Have you got something for the pain until we can get back to land?" Daniel asked. "We need to get her to a doctor as soon as possible."

"Yes, I have something that will help, but a doctor? I don't know where we're going to find one, do you, Daniel? Maybe once we find my brother, he might know. But we've got at least four days and nights of sailing just to reach the Louisiana coast. Then, we've got to make our way upriver, and hope that Keith is still around. It's going to be up to us to help her get through this. I think you can forget about doctors. Give me a hand and let's get her into that bunk, and then I'll give her something to knock out the pain."

When they had her situated, Eric told Shauna to hang in there. "You're probably not going to enjoy the passage, and you won't be hauling on any sheets or halyards, but you'll survive. Just try to get some rest. We can handle everything else. I'm going back topsides to give Dad a hand."

By the time Eric was back on deck, Bart and Jonathan had *Dreamtime* well underway with the sails set and the engine running at cruising speed. The two fishing boats were far out of rifle range now, the second one apparently dead in the water and adrift while the first was running off to the south as if it were on autopilot.

"That grenade you hit that one with must have killed everybody in the pilothouse," Bart said. "No one has touched the throttle since and the helm must be stuck. Looks to me like she's headed to the Yucatan."

"Good!" Eric said. "If there's anyone left on the other one, they must have lost interest in us, huh?"

"It sure seems that way. Jonathan told me about Shauna's wounds. What do you think, son?"

"That she's pretty lucky, considering. Clean entry and exit through the upper arm, so no bullet to dig out, and no vitals hit. Her right hand is pretty messed up though and it may not ever be the same. The incoming round almost went right up her gun barrel. It ripped through her hand and the pistol grip *and* her shoulder. The exit wasn't much bigger than the entry though, so it had to be a jacketed round and it didn't tumble much, if any."

"Bullets can do weird things, can't they son?"

"You got that right. What about other damage? We took quite a few rounds from the sound of it. Have you checked everything?"

"Yeah, and I didn't find anything critical. Several small holes through the coamings and cabin sides, one shattered port light in the aft cabin and some more holes in the starboard topsides—all high above the waterline though as far as I can tell. There's nothing we can't patch up later, after we get across.

Eric glanced ahead, noting that Bart was still steering directly into the sun.

"I figured I would stay on this course until dark. It won't hurt anything and if there is anyone still alive aboard either of those boats that might get a notion to follow us, they'll think this is still our heading. Once it gets good and dark we'll keep our lights out and then turn back north. I figure the whole deviation won't set us west more than 25 or 30 miles, tops."

"West is good in my book," Eric said. "The more distance we put between ourselves and the Florida peninsula, the better. I guess Daniel was right all along to worry about those bastards following us. It still doesn't make a whole lot of sense that they would waste that much fuel though, when they could have taken what they wanted before they let us out."

"Nothing makes a whole lot of sense anymore, son. They probably got to thinking about it, seeing us leave like that. Probably got 'em wondering what else we had. I'm sure they saw Shauna too, but I can't see that they'd go to all that trouble for a woman."

"No, but it would be a bonus on top of whatever else they took. They probably figured all we had to defend ourselves was a handgun or two… maybe a shotgun. I guess they weren't expecting grenades and automatic rifle fire, the worthless bastards."

"Well, they paid dearly for their mistake, that's for sure."

"Yeah. I just hate that Shauna had to pay too. I'm going to go check on her again; make sure the bleeding is still under control."

When Eric went below Daniel was sitting beside his wife, holding her good hand in both of his. Andrew sat opposite them on the other settee berth, still clearly shook up over what had happened.

"It's going to be okay, Andrew," Eric said. "Those bad men can't hurt us now and they're far behind us. Why don't you go up on deck and watch the sunset with Jonathan and Bart? It's going to be pretty spectacular in just a few minutes."

"I don't want to. I don't want to be out here on this boat anymore. I wish we'd just stayed at Bart's house on the river now."

"I understand, Andrew, but the danger is behind us now. Those men followed us out here, but they can't hurt us now, and no one else knows where we are. It'll be dark soon, and our boat is the only one around."

"Are all the bad guys dead? Did you shoot every single one of them?"

"Yes, I'm pretty sure they are. Even if some of them aren't, they won't mess with us again. We're going to be fine. Your stepmom is hurt, but it's not real serious. She's going to be okay."

"Why did she have to be the one to get shot? She's not even a soldier like you. It wouldn't have hurt you as much. It's not even fair."

"No, it isn't fair, Andrew, and I wish it *had* been me instead of her. But things like that are just random. I doubt anyone on board that other boat was aiming at her specifically. They were just shooting at our boat and that one bullet happened to find her. But it's a wound that will heal, Andrew, and she did her part to help me and Bart and Jonathan win the battle. You should be proud of her. Now go check out that sunset. Trust me, you don't want to miss it."

When Andrew went up the ladder, Eric turned to Daniel and Shauna. "I heard what you told him," Shauna said. "Is it really safe now? Are you sure they won't still follow us?"

"I'm pretty sure of it. One boat is running off to the south on autopilot. The other one seems to be dead in the water, and it'll be dark soon. They'll never find us again even if they were able to try. How is the pain? Has the morphine kicked in yet?"

"I guess so. I can't even move my hand though. Will it ever be normal again?"

"I don't know. You may have some shattered bones and nerve damage. It'll take some time to know for sure. The main thing is that it didn't hit any vital organs and you're not losing any more blood."

76

"I feel like I lost a lot. I feel really weak. I feel like I'm going to be sick."

"You lost a good bit, but that heavy dose of pain meds will make you feel weird too. You need to just rest and stop worrying and stop trying to talk. Sleep for now while it's working. You'll wake up when it wears off, trust me, but there's more where that came from, so don't sweat it. You can have all you need."

"She shouldn't have been out there at all," Daniel said, when Eric got up to go back on deck. "What were you thinking, putting my wife in that kind of danger?"

"I'm not the one who put her in danger, Daniel. Those men who were planning to attack us did. Shauna was out there because she could be and wanted to be. You could have taken her place, but she has the skills and you don't. I'm as sorry as you are that she got hit, believe me, but it could have been any one of us, just like I told Andrew. Bullets in a firefight don't have anyone's name on them; they're simply addressed to 'whomever it may concern'. That's just the reality of it. And the reality of this situation that we find ourselves in is that we'll probably be facing more of them sooner or later. It's time for you to accept that, Daniel, because that's the way it is now and there's nothing you or I or anyone else can do to change it. If you want to survive as long as possible, then I suggest getting into the mindset to take charge of your own protection. You can't sit on the sidelines and let others take the risks for you any longer. That's not the way it works. All of us that were out there today could have been wounded worse than Shauna or even killed. Where would that have left you and Andrew?"

"Okay, okay! I know I'm a total failure when it comes to this stuff! It's not my fault that I don't have those skills because I never needed them before. I don't have the kind of background you do. I didn't grow up in a family that went hunting or target shooting for sport. We didn't have guns in our house, and you know I was never in the military. All I know about guns is what your father showed Andrew and me before you came back. I know I need to know how to use them, but we just didn't get a chance."

"I understand. Your background doesn't matter now though. All you can do is move forward. I've seen lots of new recruits come in with no more experience than you. With proper training, they often shoot as well as anyone— sometimes better because they didn't pick up bad habits from an uninformed teacher. You and Andrew have to start somewhere, so let's start tomorrow morning. We can do some live fire training right here on the boat while we're underway. We'll throw some bottles or something overboard for targets. I want you both to be ready before we have another encounter, because next time we may not be so lucky."

Seven

ERIC RELIEVED BART AFTER sunset and assured his father he would maintain their west-southwest course for a couple more hours before turning back north on the heading for Louisiana. The two fishing boats had dropped below the horizon in the wake before it was too dark to see them, and Eric was confident they were no longer a threat. All they had to do now was keep a sharp lookout for other vessels to avoid a collision, but they had seen nothing else since they'd left Florida. As long as they were far from the coast, Eric doubted they would. Commerce had been severely disrupted by what was happening in the U.S., and freighter traffic in and out had likely ground to a halt. Jonathan and Eric were alone in the cockpit, while Bart tried to sleep and Daniel and Andrew looked after Shauna.

"I guess we're lucky we made it out here at all," Jonathan said. "They could have refused to open that blockade and killed us then and there. I guess they didn't want to make it obvious, did they? They must have people around there fooled, making them think they're protecting everybody."

"I think that was probably their intention in the beginning," Eric said. "They probably were just a group of local fishermen and boat owners who got together to defend the community. But things aren't getting any better. Resources are running out and they've probably figured out by now that it's not going to be easy to get what they need to survive. We came along and presented a target of opportunity—a temptation they couldn't resist. Now, when those two boats don't show up again, I'll bet the rest of the men at that blockade are going to think the men aboard them found even more loot on our boat than they'd hoped for and cut out on them. They're going to be pissed by tomorrow, when it's clear they aren't coming back. They'll wish they had just robbed us before they let us out. It's little too late though!"

"Yeah. It's kind of scary to think about how desperate everyone has gotten. There's no telling what we're going to run into up there in Louisiana, is there?"

"No, but one thing the area where Keith lives has going for it is that it never was as crowded as most of south Florida. The Atchafalaya swamp is about as big as the Everglades and probably just as wild, even though it's not a national park or anything. That's not to say it's not going to be dangerous though. Folks that live out in those areas have always preferred to be left alone. I don't imagine they're going to be very inviting to strangers now, but if we just keep to the river and mind our business, maybe they'll let us pass."

"I hope your brother's still there after we go all that way to find him."

"Me too, Jonathan. I have a feeling he will be, at least if he's still alive. He might have been called up with his department to help out with the riots and stuff before the hurricane, but I'd imagine that he's been laying low since then. If the infrastructure was hit as hard as it was in Florida, St. Martin Parish is going to have enough troubles of its own. I don't think they'll be working over in New Orleans or Baton Rouge at this stage. Keith is going to be working from his home base if he's working at all. He's not going to want to leave Lynn alone for long."

"And you said they don't have any kids, right?"

"No, it's just the two of them, but Lynn comes from a big enough family that they have so many nieces and nephews they don't need kids of their own. You'll like his place. It's a lot like my Dad's place on the Caloosahatchee, but even more rustic and out of the way. It was originally going to be their weekend camp, but they both liked it out there so much they decided it was the only home they needed. The whole cabin is made of reclaimed sinker cypress that Keith and his brother-in-law pulled out of the river and milled themselves. It's elevated a good ten feet or so on pilings too, like most of the camps in those parts. Just like at Dad's place, he's got a boat dock right out back, with access to all the wetlands of south Louisiana that can be reached by navigable water. His work often starts right off that dock, in his sheriff's department patrol boat, or at least it used to."

"Sounds like a sweet setup, dude. How did he end up there with you guys growing up in Florida? Is that where his wife is from?"

"Yep. She's full-blooded Cajun, and a hot little thing too. I like her a lot. She's very cool. Keith met her on a road trip through there when he got out of the Marines and that's where he's been ever since."

"Wow, he was in the Marines? You were a SEAL, and your dad was in Vietnam! You guys are just a whole family of badasses! Did your brother ever fight in any wars?"

"Oh yeah. He was in Iraq, so he's seen plenty of combat, and I'm sure he's had some encounters as a deputy too; even before the shit started hitting the fan in this country."

"I'll bet he's going to be surprised and happy to see you and your dad show up there. It's too bad Megan's not already with you, or y'all could all just stay there."

"Yeah, I won't be hanging around for long, I can assure you of that. Boulder, Colorado is a long way from south Louisiana when you can't even drive it, much less hop a plane. I hope Keith has a better idea than taking a riverboat up the Mississippi, but if he does, I don't know what it would be."

It was Bart who had suggested that traveling part of the way north and west by river might be a good idea. Bart had been in contact with Keith via ham radio before the hurricane, and Keith had told him that most of the fuel that was still being distributed from the storage facilities and refineries on the Gulf coast was now transported by barge. It was the safest way to move it, due to dangers of the roadways, where vehicles could be stopped or attacked at any point by bandits or various factions fighting over territory. Even the towboats and barges running the rivers were subject to ambush though, and that's why Bart figured there were plenty of openings for experienced security contractors like Eric. If he could work his passage or even if he had to pay for the ride, he could likely get north to St. Louis and then west as far as possible on the Missouri before cutting off to overland the rest of the way to Boulder. It would be a relatively slow means of travel, but slow and sure was better than not getting there at all.

Eric knew Shauna wanted to go too, and convincing her to stay behind would have been impossible before she got shot. But he was certain it wouldn't have worked out anyway. He didn't need Daniel tagging along, incompetent and in the way, and the man would flip out at the thought of Shauna going off on such a journey with her ex-husband without him. Now that she was wounded, it was out of the question, and in way, Eric was relieved. The more he was around her, the more the old feelings for her resurfaced, and he knew her presence would compromise his mission because he would be constantly looking out for her. She wouldn't be able to argue with him now when he told her she would have to wait at Keith and Lynn's. With her hand in that condition, it would be a long time before she could handle a weapon again, and Eric wasn't taking anyone who couldn't fight. He had already been thinking about it before today's incident and figured he'd probably be better off going alone. Keith would want to help, and he was certainly competent, assuming nothing had happened to him, but Eric wasn't sure how Lynn would feel about it, and depending on how things had played out there in the parish, his brother could still be carrying out his duties with the department. That left Bart and Jonathan, and Eric had no plans to ask either of them to come. His father was capable but he was also 69 years old and would slow him down even if he was in great shape for his age. Jonathan was young and probably willing, but inexperienced and untrained. Eric didn't expect him to take such a risk and he didn't feel that he owed the kid anything else but a ride to the Atchafalaya and maybe a fishing boat if they could find one.

The prospect of going alone didn't really bother him anyway. It would be easier for one man to keep a low profile moving cross-country, and he would only have himself to worry about. When he found Megan, he'd a have a whole new set of problems getting her back to the boat so they could leave for good, but that was something to worry about then, and not now. As he considered that, Eric decided now wasn't the time to worry at all. They were out of south Florida and their pursuers were defeated. Shauna would recover, even without professional medical care just as long as she didn't get an infection. The boat Bart had chosen was fantastic, and Eric had full confidence it would get them where they wanted to go. He stayed on deck the rest of the night, alternating watches with Jonathan until Bart came back out at 0300 hours.

"She's sleeping now, but she's been in a lot of pain," he said, when Eric asked how Shauna was doing. "I feel for her. That hand's got to hurt!"

When daylight returned, Eric went below to change her dressings and inspect the wounds. The clotting agent had done a good job of quickly stopping the bleeding, just as Eric had expected, having successfully used the same dressings to seal even bigger holes. Shauna winced as he unwrapped her hand though, and as he expected, it looked far worse than her upper arm. There was little he could do about the shattered bones, other than keep the hand wrapped and mostly immobilized.

"Have you seen any more boats?" she asked as he finished the new dressings. "Any sign of those two during the night?"

"No. Nothing new and the last we saw of them was before dark yesterday. We don't have to worry about those men any longer. I doubt we'll run into marine traffic before we close on the coast. I want to take advantage of the smooth conditions this morning to give Daniel and Andrew a bit of firearms training. With you out of commission, I want to make sure they can shoot before we make landfall." Eric turned to Shauna's husband and stepson: "Are you guys ready? If so, let's get started. I'm going to need some sleep in a couple of hours."

The two days and nights that followed gave Eric plenty of time to get in several short shooting sessions with Daniel and Andrew. Starting them out on the SKS rifle, he took them through the differences in the AK, the M4 and the various shotguns they had aboard. Then they checked out on the Glock 19 and got some time on one of Bart's .45 autos as well as a .357 Magnum revolver. It helped to pass the time on the otherwise uneventful passage, and made Eric feel much better, transforming two passengers into at least beginner marksmen who could attempt to do their part if they got into another firefight.

By the morning of the third day at sea, they were sailing through the deep-water oilfields more than a hundred miles south of the mouth of the Mississippi River. The remote drilling platforms out here were abandoned now, of course. Eric knew they would have been evacuated for a hurricane in

86

normal times, but they had likely shutdown long before that due to the economic collapse brought about by the insurrection. With GPS satellites disabled and most of these rigs unlit, it was an extremely dangerous place to sail. The most up to date paper charts Bart had been able to find among the vessels in his boatyard before they left were already two years old, and in the oilfield that made them very dated. In the year and a half prior to the unraveling of the country, the industry had still been strong, and new rigs would have been put into place or moved around for exploratory drilling. That meant there were structures out there not indicated on those paper charts, and avoiding them—especially at night—required extreme diligence from the entire crew of *Dreamtime*.

The onboard radar was helpful, at least for picking out the largest structures above the surface with a good signature, but it wasn't enough when a band of heavy thunderstorms rolled in from the west. Bart said it wasn't worth the risk to keep sailing until the weather passed.

"Anywhere in the vicinity of these rigs there's no telling what kind of obstructions we're liable to run into. There's pipe and all kinds of stuff just under the surface, waiting to ruin our day. I say we ought to do our best to just hold position right here where we have a point of reference until it clears up enough to move on."

Bart pointed to the two drilling platforms less than a mile apart that they were approximately half way between. The one to the west quickly disappeared in sheets of rain as the storm swept towards them, but with the engine running just fast enough to maintain steerage, Bart kept *Dreamtime* in position by making slow circles until the storm passed and they could see both derricks again. More heavy rain greeted them several times as the stormy afternoon wore on, and each time they had to reduce speed or stop to avoid the risk of blindly pushing on in such a dangerous area. When the skies finally cleared well after dark, they were able to sail again, but only with at least two of the crew on deck at all times, keeping a sharp watch. Eric and Jonathan were sharing this duty at the bow, while Daniel took a turn at the helm, allowing Bart to get some sleep.

"I had no idea there were so many of these rigs out here," Jonathan said. "This must have been like sailing through a city back when they were all working and lit up at night."

"I imagine it would have been. I've had friends over the years that worked the rigs out here. The oil field here is vast. All you have to do is look at the charts to see it; and there's no telling how many new ones there are since those were printed."

"And now they've all been abandoned. I wonder how long it's going to be until all the oil in the country runs out?

It's already impossible for most people to get any gas. What's going to happen when it's all gone?"

"It'll take some time to use up all the reserves, and there may be a limited amount coming in from overseas, but it probably won't make a difference in the availability of gasoline and diesel for the general public. Whoever is in control of the oil now will do their best to keep it that way. They'll control it so they can control people's movements, as well as the price, which will be through the roof for the foreseeable future. If things ever stabilize later, they'll make a killing."

"I'll bet. And I'll bet there'll be plenty of actual killings over it too. I'm sure there already has been."

"No doubt about it. Moving fuel has got to be one of the most dangerous jobs there is by now. That's why they're moving it by riverboat, if they're still moving it at all. I imagine my Dad is right about the opportunities for my kind of work on those boats."

"Man, I wish I could qualify for a job like that!"

"Are you sure about that, Jonathan? Did you really enjoy getting shot at on board a boat with nowhere to go the other day? It was bad enough that Shauna got hit. It could have been any of us though. It's a good way to end up dead, I'll tell you that."

"Well, you've been doing that shit for years, and you're not dead yet. What kept you going back to it, even though you had a wife and daughter at home?"

"Stupidity!" Eric said. "Look at me and learn from my mistakes. You don't want to do what I did, that's for sure. Find yourself a nice place to hole up in the swamp when we get there and stick to fishing. You don't need to try and earn money anyway because it's pretty much worthless right now."

"I can live off of my fishing, that's a fact, and probably catch enough to trade for any other goods I need if that Atchafalaya River is like you and your old man say it is. I'm damned good at it; you know that. But still, I think it'll get boring after while. I'd like to do what I can to fight back against all those idiots trying to tear our country apart. It's not any different than when you enlisted to go fight the terrorists overseas. You felt a calling to do it, didn't you, a sense of duty to your country? I can't see where you totally regret it, even if you say you do. If you did, you could have quit a long time ago, but you didn't."

"It was a different world then. I believed in what I was doing. I still don't know the full extent of what's happened here until I see more of it for myself, but I've got a feeling it can never go back to the way it was. Like I told you the first day we met, I'm here to find my daughter and get her and the rest of my family out. That other stuff is no longer my problem."

Eight

AFTER A NIGHT OF intense and exhausting watch keeping, traversing the offshore oil fields without a working GPS and electronic charts, the final day of *Dreamtime's* Gulf voyage dawned fair and clear. Based on their dead reckoning calculations and confirmed by a U.S. Coast Guard tower marker they identified on the paper charts, Eric and Bart estimated they were within 30 miles of the Louisiana coast near the mouth of the Atchafalaya River.

Neither of them had ever been to this coast, though they had both visited Keith and Lynn at their bayou-front home some 50 miles upriver. That part of the Atchafalaya to the north was a different world—a watery wilderness of classic Louisiana cypress swamp and bottomland hardwood forest. The coast, however, was flat and utterly featureless, even more devoid of natural landmarks than most of south Florida and barely above sea level. Most of it consisted of open expanses of salt marsh, broken only by drilling platforms and related oil field infrastructure. Knowing this, Eric didn't expect to be able to pick out the details of the river entrance until they were within a couple of miles. That was just the nature of approaching this type of low-lying coast by boat. By the time they were that close, the tall masts of *Dreamtime* would also be visible to anyone who happened to be ashore there, although it seemed doubtful anyone would be since the passage of the hurricane. Even a modest storm surge would have put the entire area underwater, and exposure to such events was the main reason there was so little development along this coast in the first place. Only a few hardy communities like Grande Isle to the east managed to persist here long-term, rebuilding each time a major storm left them in ruin. It was doubtful any of those places would make a comeback from this one though; not without the outside help that was as unlikely to arrive here as it was in south Florida. Survivors in such places, if there were any, had surely moved on to more habitable environments; at least that's what Eric and Bart assumed. They would know for sure soon enough.

Approaching any coast in the aftermath of a hurricane was dangerous from a navigational standpoint, regardless of the presence or lack thereof of survivors. Channel markers would likely be destroyed or moved out of their correct positions. Sunken vessels and structural debris swept offshore by the storm surge would be everywhere, hidden beneath the murky brown waters near shore and impossible to detect until it was too late. They would have to navigate by visual cues alone, keeping a sharp lookout and reading the surface of the water to try and pick up the signs of such hazards in time to avoid them. It would require all hands on deck—with only Shauna getting a pass, but after they were in the river, the days and nights of alternating watches and around the clock sailing were over. There would be no nighttime navigation there. They would be forced to find a place to anchor before it got dark, as it would be far too risky to run the confined and winding river channel at night. Bart suggested that they anchor as soon as they were within the mouth anyway, so that they could go ahead and lower the masts. They couldn't get under the bridges at Morgan City with them up, and that was only some twenty miles upriver. The highway bridge there had a vertical clearance of just 30 feet according to the charts, and they had to assume that it would be permanently closed. There was also a railroad bridge with an even lower clearance. Beyond that, they had no idea, because that was where the marine charts ended, with everything upstream covered on inland navigation charts, of which they had none. Bart said that some of the inland railroad swing bridges could be even lower, with barely enough clearance to get under even with the spars down.

"Since they built them to swing open, they didn't bother making them high enough for much else besides small fishing boats to go under. In a lot of places they tend to keep them open all the time except when a train is scheduled to arrive. But they could all be locked down now and left that way. Or they could be using them again by now, who knows? I think we ought to expect them to be closed though, and have the boat ready to go under beforehand. I'd rather not be sitting within sight of a bridge while we're busy getting the masts down. It would leave us too vulnerable to an attack."

"I agree," Eric said. "Let's find a place to anchor when we reach the coast and get it done. It looks like there are several small islands around the mouth of the river." Eric pointed as he and Bart studied the chart. "They're probably not much of anything but marsh, but they might provide us enough shelter to stop and get things sorted for the trip upriver."

"I imagine so," Bart said. "All we need is enough of a lee that she won't be rolling. Then we can drop those spars and get a good night's rest while we're there."

When they were finally close enough to see the coast first-hand, picking out the river mouth was just as difficult as Eric had deduced it would be from the chart. The outlying marsh islands were so low against the backdrop of the equally low mainland that they were practically indistinguishable. With no GPS waypoints to guide them in, it would be nearly impossible to find the river without running aground, unless they could find some channel markers.

With Bart steering, Eric and Jonathan moved to the bow, each of them carrying a pair of binoculars with which to scan the horizon ahead. The first markers they spotted that correlated to the chart were a pair of pilings standing in a gap amidst a cluster of the small, grassy islands. There was a red triangle on the one to starboard and a green square on the one to port, just as it should be to mark a channel entrance from sea. Eric waved Bart forward until he could read the numbers: "30" for the red one and "29" for the green. Calling them back to his father, he waited for Bart to confirm by the chart that yes; these were indeed part of the line of markers leading into the Atchafalaya. There should have been more of them offshore, but apparently they had been swept away by the hurricane storm surge. Looking to the north, Eric could see more of them that way, though some were missing their red or green signs and many were leaning over at an angle. Regardless, they provided enough clues to guide them into the river, and that was a good thing, because without them the marsh islands and channels intercepting them would have been an impossibly confusing maze.

As Bart guided *Dreamtime* straight ahead through the transition from open water to the calm of the river mouth, evidence of the storm's passing became apparent everywhere. There was so much debris washed up at the water's edge in great drifts that it looked like the work of bulldozers rearranging trash at a landfill.

"The storm surge must have carried all this stuff out here when it receded," Bart said. "It didn't come from here, because there wasn't much here to begin with. I suppose it could have washed down from Morgan City or even from over at Grand Isle or somewhere."

"Wherever it came from, it confirms what Jonathan and I heard from that fellow we passed off the Everglades. He said the worst of the damage was west of New Orleans. It looks like he was right. I have no doubt now that Keith and Lynn got hit pretty hard, considering they're not all that far north of here."

"Yeah, you're probably right. We'll have a pretty good idea how bad it was when we get to Morgan City. I don't think there's anything between here and there that would do much to weaken a hurricane. After seeing this, I imagine that place got clobbered."

The stuff littering the riverbanks included every imaginable artifact of modern life, from pieces of roofing and siding to doors and large appliances like refrigerators and dryers, now half-buried in the muddy banks. Lighter items, such as couch cushions, mattresses and articles of clothing were scattered farther from the water throughout the tall marsh grass, mixed in with plastic toys, bottles and everything else that would float on a storm surge. Eric could only imagine the fury of the waves here at the time of the hurricane's peak intensity. Everything in sight would have been completely submerged, with breaking seas from the open Gulf rolling in unimpeded. Unless they had adequate warning and the means to evacuate, the death toll among residents in this entire region probably exceeded any storm in recent history and conditions for the survivors would be miserable. There was little reason for anyone to remain here along the lower reaches of the river after that, so Eric doubted they would encounter survivors until they went farther upstream. When they came to a small opening off the main channel that was big enough for the schooner, he suggested they drop anchor there to prepare the boat for the next leg.

"I'd like to do it right here where we have good visibility upriver *and* out to sea. If anyone comes along, we'll have plenty of warning. We'll still keep a watch posted after dark tonight, but everyone should be able to get some solid rest before we head upriver tomorrow."

"It feels weird all of a sudden, now that the boat's not rolling constantly," Jonathan said.

"Yeah, you had just enough time to get your sea legs, and now we've made landfall. I'll bet Daniel won't be complaining though," Eric said. "He was looking pretty green that first day out, until the excitement of all that gunfire cured him of it!"

"Works every time, doesn't it, son?" Bart said.

"Yeah, getting shot at certainly changes a man's perspective on things. I think he's finally starting to wake up to how things are now. He certainly hasn't been complaining as much after what happened to Shauna." Daniel and Andrew were both off watch and sleeping down below at the moment, so Eric could speak freely.

"Learning how to shoot probably has a lot to do with it too. He's bound to feel a little better about himself now. I reckon it took seeing his wife get hit to make him realize he can't sit out the next fight."

Daniel and Andrew couldn't sit out the work that had to be done next either. As soon as the anchor was set, Eric went below to wake them. It would take all hands to remove the sails and running rigging and stow everything away in preparation for dropping the spars. Eric wanted to get it done today so they could get an early start the next morning as soon as it was light enough to safely navigate.

"I'm sorry I can't help you guys," Shauna said, when Eric headed back up the ladder.

"You've got a good excuse Shauna, so you get a pass. How are you feeling?" Eric didn't really have to ask, because he knew she was still in a lot of pain, made bearable only by medication. Her right hand was completely unusable and would be for no telling how long. For now, it was immobilized in a bandage and splint combination to keep her from bumping it and making it worse, something that was hard to avoid when the boat was offshore, the motion sometimes slamming her into the sides of her bunk. Eric had changed the bandages on the hand and upper arm often, adjusting for the swelling and checking for infection. So far, the wounds looked as good as could be expected, and she wasn't complaining, but healing was going to take time.

"I'm looking forward to a calm night. It'll be nice to sleep without having to hold on for a change."

"Yes it will. If you need something to knock you out, just let me know. I've got the good stuff in my kit. We'll get started early tomorrow. The rest of the way to Keith's should be smooth going, at least as far as the sailing is concerned."

"I hope you're right, Eric."

Eric didn't want Shauna to worry, but after all they'd been though, they both knew they could run into almost anything upriver. She would no more turn back than he would though, no matter what they were facing, because getting to Keith's was the necessary next step in the main objective, which was to find Megan and get her out of danger. If Keith and Lynn were not there for some reason, then they would formulate a plan B, but that wasn't something to worry about now.

Before they lowered the mainmast, which was the one upon which the marine radio antenna was mounted, Bart said he wanted to see if they could possibly raise Keith on the VHF band. "I know it's a long shot he'll be listening, but if he happens to be out patrolling the river in his boat, there's a chance he may be monitoring Channel 16."

"Can you really reach out that far on VHF?" Eric knew that Bart had added a power output booster to *Dreamtime's* radio that was supposed to greatly increase the normal 25-

watt transmitter signal. He'd taken it off of another vessel in the boatyard, saying it wasn't normally legal anywhere but in international waters, but that it might come in handy now.

"I've never tried it, but they say you can. With that extra-tall antenna at the top of the mast and nothing much in the way, it ought to reach him. We won't know for sure, of course, because he won't be able to call us back, but it's worth a shot."

"Just as long as it doesn't get picked up by somebody we'd rather not give our location to."

"Don't worry about that. I'm not going to be too specific, but I'll make sure Keith knows it's me calling, even if he doesn't recognize my voice." Bart keyed the mic and began speaking:

"St Martin Parish S.O., St. Martin Parish S.O…. This is the sailing vessel *Dreamtime*, Captain Bart Branson, inbound from the Caloosahatchee River, over…."

Eric smiled. Keith would be shocked if he indeed heard that. To anyone else, it would be utterly confusing. The Caloosahatchee was so far from here that it would never come up in normal vessel chatter over the radio. Most locals may not have even heard of it. Anyone picking up the message might assume it was some kind of weird, long distance skip, except that he was asking for a specific sheriff's department in the region. Regardless of what they thought, no one would know where the call came from. Bart waited several minutes and when there was no answer, repeated his transmission three more times, specifically asking for Deputy Branson in those last attempts.

"I reckon that'll do it. Like I said, he may or may not be monitoring the channel. Either way, it's time to shut it down and drop those masts. The sooner we do that, the sooner we can get up there and talk to him in person."

It took the bulk of the afternoon, but before sunset *Dreamtime* had been converted from an ocean sailor to a power river cruiser. With both masts down and in the horizontal position, moving about on deck was going to be a bit awkward, as they had to duck under them to cross from port to starboard and vice versa, but that was an inconvenience they would have to put up with. Aside from effortlessly slipping under low bridges, there were other advantages to dropping the spars.

"We'll have a much lower profile now," Bart said, "and that's a good thing, especially out here in the marsh. But it'll be good for rounding those blind river bends once we reach the woods too."

Eric agreed that Bart had a good point. The two masts, the main standing over forty feet tall, would be visible for a long way. With them down, the highest part of the vessel was maybe eight feet above the waterline—a significant difference indeed when they might need to slip into a side channel or bayou to stay out of sight of river traffic. The only downside to the arrangement was that they were relying solely on the engine now, with no alternative propulsion, but Eric wasn't overly concerned about it, and neither was Bart. The Perkins had performed flawlessly in the Gulf and there was no reason to doubt that it would push *Dreamtime* upriver and back again when it was time to return to sea. They still had more than enough fuel to motor all the way to Keith's place and back to the coast again with plenty of reserve to spare, thanks to all the plastic Jerry cans lashed to the rails both port and starboard, but Eric and Bart both preferred to have as much of that as possible in the internal tanks. Eric handed Jonathan the fuel funnel and assigned him the task of topping them off from the cans.

"Get Andrew to hold this for you while you pour. Now that we're anchored, it ought to be easier to do without spilling any, so take your time." They topped up once midway through the passage, when it was a lot trickier due to the motion. There was more than enough left for a second refill and it was better to do it now while nothing was happening than later when it might be critical to have full tanks.

Nighttime in the river delta was eerily quiet, with only the sound of the southerly breeze rustling through the marsh grass surrounding them and no water rushing past the hull for the first time in days. It was as dark here as it had been on the open Gulf, with no manmade lights in sight; the oil rigs that were visible in the daylight all abandoned now and unlit. Bart figured it was unlikely there'd be any boat traffic passing through the lower river at night, and maybe not even in the daytime. The Gulf Intracoastal Waterway intersected the Atchafalaya just upriver at Morgan City, and he felt that would be the route the barges would use if they were still moving fuel from Texas to the north.

They were to find out that was not necessarily the case though after they got underway to head upriver the next morning. Eric was at the helm with his father and Daniel in the cockpit next to him, while Jonathan and Andrew kept lookout from the bow. They had rounded a slight bend to the northeast and were now following a straight section where the river channel turned back due north when a tow pushing a dozen barges suddenly appeared around the bend from astern. With the engines of the tow so far back behind all those barges and the noise of the old Perkins rumbling below their own decks, no one on board had heard a thing. Daniel noticed the huge vessel first, when he glanced back over their stern rail.

"They're coming up on us really fast," he said. "What can we do?"

"Stay out of the way, is the main thing," Eric said. "He's got plenty of room to pass us as long as we're not in the middle of the channel."

"Are you sure he even wants to pass? What if they're planning to attack us like the men on those two fishing boats?"

"They're not out to attack anybody," Bart said. "They're probably moving fuel or something like that. I guess I was wrong to assume they wouldn't enter the river from the Gulf though."

Eric began angling off to port from the center of the channel, where he'd been running for the best chance of avoiding submerged debris. With the Perkins at nearly full throttle, *Dreamtime* was making hull speed at just over eight knots as the tide was nearly at peak high and there was little current working for or against them. The tow was probably making twelve knots though, and rapidly gaining on them. Eric was sure the captain could see the schooner clearly by now, even with the masts down, but the blunt prows of the barges, rafted three across and four deep, were still coming right at them, despite Eric's evasive maneuver.

"What the hell is he doing?" Bart asked. "He's got more than enough room to get by without running us clear out of the damned channel!"

"I think he's trying to run over us on purpose!" Daniel said, before shouting to Andrew to get back to the cockpit.

"I don't think he wants to actually hit us," Eric said, "but he damned sure wants us out of the way, and a lot more than necessary if you ask me."

"There's a couple of fellows moving forward on those barges," Bart said, as he studied the approaching vessel through the binoculars. "It looks like they're armed, too."

"Probably security, like Keith said. Just watch them closely. I'm going to ease over a bit more."

Eric didn't like edging out of the channel at full speed, but if he backed down on the throttle the schooner might not get out of the way in time. Jonathan was still at the bow looking for obstructions, but the muddy brown waters of the river obscured from view anything more than a few inches below the surface. Eric had moved just outside one of the remaining green channel markers as the steel topsides of the barges slid by, the two men at the bows studying them closely but not making any threatening gestures with their rifles. Eric was already reaching for the throttle to reduce speed when suddenly there was a crashing impact that shook the entire vessel from bow to stern. *Dreamtime's* hull seemed to climb partially out of the water, while at the same time listing sharply to port before slamming to a stop. The sudden impact threw everyone but Eric off their feet, and he only managed to avoid it because he was hanging onto the wheel. He heard Shauna scream from down below and looking forward saw that Jonathan had apparently gone over the bow rail and into the river.

The line of barges sliced past the suddenly grounded schooner from just yards away and when the tow pushing them was adjacent, a long, obnoxious blast sounded from the horn to add to the insult. Whoever that bastard at the helm was, he didn't care that he'd forced them aground, and Eric realized that Daniel was right—he would have just as soon run them down if they hadn't gotten out of the way in time, and they barely had.

Nine

KEITH BRANSON WAS ABOUT to resume his hammering when the VHF radio once again broke silence on Channel 16. He'd been in the middle of nailing down another section of roof decking when the first call came, and had missed nearly every word of it before he realized what it was and stopped to listen. The transmission could have been anything and was probably just normal navigation-related chatter between a couple of passing towboat captains on the nearby river, but Keith wanted to be sure. He had waited a minute or two in silence, but it was already late afternoon and he had work to do. Those nails weren't going to drive themselves, and he was ready to get back at it when he heard that second call suddenly come through. This time it was loud and clear.

Listening carefully to every word, Keith stared across the yard to his patrol boat tied up at the dock there, and then he dropped the hammer into the loop of his tool belt and quickly descended the ladder to the ground. He had just reached the dock when the voice sounded through the radio speaker again, repeating the previous call word-for-word.

Keith hopped into the boat and grabbed the microphone from its clip on the panel of the center console, his own voice trembling a bit as he answered.

"Vessel calling St. Martin Parish S.O., this is Deputy Branson, St. Martin Parish S.O...."

Keith turned the volume on the receiver to wide open and waited. When there was no answer, he tried again.

"Vessel calling St. Martin Parish S.O. on VHF Channel 16, this is Deputy Keith Branson, St. Martin Parish Sheriff's Department. Do you read me? Is that really you, Dad?"

No reply. Keith waited quietly for a moment before trying again, but still there was nothing.... His attempts to answer the unexpected call apparently weren't getting through, but it didn't matter; *this was still huge!* Keith took a few deep breaths to calm down a little as he switched on the ignition and pushed the power tilt controls to lower the twin 150-hp Mercury outboards into the water. His thoughts raced as he started the engines to let them warm up while he went to grab what he needed out of the house.

When he was back aboard the boat, he secured his department-issued M4 in its rack on the side of the center console and put his small go-bag in the locker under one of the seats. His duty pistol never left his side of course, even while he was working on the house, but heading out anywhere in the boat or on the roads these days, he always took the rifle and plenty of spare mags for it. With the dock lines cast off, Keith pushed the twenty-one foot aluminum vessel away from the pilings with his boathook and shifted the engines into gear.

He didn't know how it was possible, but the call he'd just received on the radio was real. He might have dismissed it as his imagination if it hadn't been repeated twice more after it got his attention. *How many weeks had it been since he'd last heard that voice… seven… probably closer to eight?* It seemed surreal that it could have been that long, but Keith knew it had. His memories of those past weeks were as jumbled and disarrayed as the destruction left behind by the hurricane. He'd spent most of them in a daze, struggling with the disbelief and pain of his loss. It would have been easier if he had died there that day as well, but he'd been too late on the scene. He forced himself to go on each day since, even though so little remained of what he'd lived for that it seemed there was hardly any point.

He still had the patrol boat and his weapons though, and there were others who needed his help that suffered as much or more. The secluded bayou hideaway where he and Lynn had built their home was still there, and although the house was badly damaged and would take lots more work to repair, it wasn't a total loss. Keith still had his tools, and materials were available to salvage or barter for. There was enough fuel in his own secure storage tank to run the outboards and his vehicles for several more weeks, and his stockpiles of food had survived intact. Keith had been relatively well prepared considering the circumstances. The events that unfolded before the beginning of summer had prompted him to think about his options, and he and Lynn had agreed it was better to be safe than sorry. Being ready for a hurricane was a given when living this close to the Gulf of Mexico, and they were already set up to weather such a storm and the resulting power outages and disruptions. No one expected to get hit by one of this magnitude with so little warning though, especially after everything else that happened recently, already putting them in a state of emergency and isolation. Because of all that, most folks in the hurricane's path were caught at a time when they were most exposed and vulnerable.

There were lots of tough and self-sufficient folks out here in the Atchafalaya River Basin that could get through about anything, but there were also many in Keith's jurisdiction that needed far more help than they were likely to get. And there were the outsiders too, with no business here at all, some of them simply desperate refugees trying to survive, and others that were part of the problem to begin with. Keith had the means to make a difference in the lives of both sorts, and he intended to carry out his sworn duties to the best of his ability, despite the crushing loss that weighed heavily upon him through every waking moment.

That call coming over the radio, as improbable as it seemed, suddenly gave Keith a renewed sense of purpose and hope. The prospect of seeing family was *exactly* what he needed right now, especially the prospect of seeing his father, who had never failed to provide sound guidance and advice. The last time Keith had spoken with him had been via ham radio, their conversation focused on the unnamed hurricane that at the time was approaching south Florida from the West Indies. They'd each picked up bits and pieces of info on the storm track as reports of it spread through the Caribbean amateur radio nets. With the federal government practically shut down and public television and radio broadcasts limited or inaccessible, few people in the path of the massive storm even knew it was coming. But having lived in south Florida for more than 30 years while operating a boatyard there, Bart Branson was well prepared for hurricanes too. The last time Keith had made contact with him, he'd said he was going to North Palm Beach to evacuate his granddaughter and former daughter-in-law, if they were still at home there. It was far safer to ride out the storm at his riverfront bungalow on the Caloosahatchee than near that exposed Atlantic coast, as the winds would likely weaken somewhat by the time it crossed the peninsula to the Gulf.

But Keith hadn't heard a word from Bart since and had no way of knowing whether or not they'd made it through safely. They had been unable to reconnect by radio due to damage to the repeater towers throughout the affected region. Cell phone networks, the Internet and other communications options were already blacked out or intermittent well before the storm arrived. The sustained winds of a major hurricane no doubt dealt a heavy blow to the infrastructure in south Florida, just as they had in this part of Louisiana. Keith didn't know for sure, but he had to assume the power grid was completely down in practically all of the southern part of his state and probably clear across south Mississippi and Alabama as well. The anarchists and disrupters had gotten what they wanted in the end, and likely far more than they actually bargained for. Keith hoped they were suffering as much as the untold number of innocents affected by their senseless acts of violence, but whether they were or not, it was too late to undo what had been done. The hurricane was a regional event. Those larger problems were nationwide, and Keith was sure the burning, looting and killing was still going on in most places. There was little chance of getting much news of it now though, especially out here on the Atchafalaya.

Keith sped up as he steered the boat down the winding bayou that would take him to the river. These waterways and the enclosing hardwood forests that surrounded them were among the few things in his world that were largely unchanged. There were downed and damaged trees, of course, and the banks were littered with debris carried in on the flood waters, but for the most part, the natural world always fared better in such storms than the things built by man. Keith found a little comfort in knowing that. The great swamp and its waterways and woods had a lot to do with why he was here in the first place. Lynn's family history in the Atchafalaya region went back for generations, and when Keith met her, it didn't take him long to understand she would not easily be uprooted, and the more time he spent with her here, the less he cared. It was easier for him to stay than to get her to move. He got his job with the sheriff's department, married her, and the two of them built their secluded bayou home that he thought they would share forever.

The events that left him alone now couldn't be undone, and though everything had changed in the world beyond the levees, at least the bayous and the river remained. The Atchafalaya's dark waters still flowed past fluted cypress trunks and muddy islands of dense willows; creating a vast stronghold of bayous, sloughs, canals and lakes accessible only by boat. And now that wilderness of isolated waterways was more cut off from the outside world than ever, with fuel in short supply and the roads leading to it too dangerous to travel. The river was the main artery through the heart of his jurisdiction now, and Keith made it his job to keep an eye on the comings and goings of those who used it.

He'd been south as far as Morgan City and the Gulf only a few times since the hurricane struck, and what he found there was the devastation and death he expected. With a direct hit from what must have been at least a Category Four storm at landfall, the outcome wasn't really surprising. Most folks living near the coast didn't get out because they had no better place to go if they even had a way to get there. They simply decided to take their chances with nature rather than face the fuel shortages, roadblocks and bandits they were sure to encounter in an evacuation attempt.

Keith helped those survivors he could find, taking some of them back upriver in his boat where they at least had a chance of finding food and fresh water. But the dead were too numerous to do anything about. Bodies were washed up at random on the riverbanks and throughout the marsh and mixed with piles of rubble in what was left of whole communities. By the time he saw all this, Keith was immune to the normal emotions such a scene would have evoked before. Though it was as bad as anything he'd encountered in the war he'd fought overseas, nothing could get to him after seeing the aftermath of what had happened on the bridge, the day he lost Lynn.

Keith hadn't been back to what was left of Morgan City in nearly a month now, after evacuating the last of the survivors he found there. He'd had enough to do to keep him busy helping his in-laws and other folks closer to home, but now he wondered if his father's call had come from somewhere down that way. Wherever it was, it was too far away to answer, and that was frustrating, but not really surprising. The VHF antenna on his patrol boat wasn't tall enough to transmit more than a few miles. Reception was always a lot better than transmission on those radios, and Bart was undoubtedly aboard a much larger vessel with a taller antenna if he had come all the way here from south Florida. Keith's best guess was that he was somewhere on the main channel of the Atchafalaya, likely already north of Morgan City.

Thinking about it as he wound his way around the bends of the bayou to the river, Keith figured things had to be really bad in Florida for Bart Branson to come all the way here by boat. The last time they'd discussed it, his old man had insisted that he was better off than most everybody down there, with his secluded little hideaway on the Caloosahatchee, but he *was* concerned about his granddaughter and her mother. There had been major riots just south of them in West Palm Beach, and it was even worse in Miami. Keith hated to think about Megan and Shauna being stranded there, but there was little he could do about it, considering the distance. Taking care of them was Eric's job, but his brother made other choices long ago, and Keith couldn't really blame Shauna for divorcing him and moving on. She was doing what she had to do to take care of herself and Megan. He just hoped they were both okay after all this.

If he had been able to get through to his father after the surprise radio call today, he would have bombarded him with all his questions: *Did he get Shauna and Megan out? Were they with him now? Had anyone heard from Eric? What about Shauna's new husband, was he with them too?* The answers would have to wait though, because so far, there was nothing to indicate that Bart had received his reply. Keith was too impatient to sit there doing nothing though, and that's why he was headed for the river now. Maybe Bart was anchored somewhere nearby, unsure of how to find Keith's property by water, as he'd only been fishing with him there once years prior. Keith would check the stretch of river nearest the bayou, and if he didn't see him there, he would run up to his brother-in-law's place on the old river channel north of the interstate and try his radio. Vic Guidry had a much taller antenna on his fishing trawler, and could certainly transmit farther than Keith could. It would be preferable to make radio contact with his father first rather than spend time running miles up and down the river looking for him without even knowing what kind of vessel he was aboard and whether or not he was in the old river or the Whiskey Bay Pilot Channel.

Keith suspected he might be aboard one of the larger motor yachts from his boatyard. Maybe he had a customer there who was based somewhere in Louisiana or Texas, and he'd caught a ride here. Or he could have arranged to come on a commercial work or freight vessel. It was even possible that he wasn't aboard a boat at all, but instead had called from one of the roads nearby, despite the fact that he'd used the VHF. In normal times it was illegal to use that frequency band for anything other than marine communications, but Bart wouldn't care about that now, and he would have certainly had access to many such radios in the boatyard he could have brought with him, including handheld units.

Keith called again as he neared the river, hoping he was getting closer and that he might get through, but there was still no reply, and when he reached the broad expanse of the Atchafalaya, he saw nothing moving either upstream or downstream as far as he could see to the next bends. He motored out to the middle of the channel and killed the engines, sitting there adrift in the lazy current as he tried the radio again:

"Vessel calling St. Martin Parish S.O., this is Deputy Branson, St. Martin Parish S.O... I repeat, this is Deputy Keith Branson, St. Martin Parish Sheriff's Department. Do you read me, Dad?"

Keith waited and tried again several more times before starting the outboards again and speeding downriver to the next bend to have a look. There was nothing in sight there either, and his calls went unanswered, so he turned the boat around to run up to the north and try the radio on Vic's boat. He had just reached his brother-in-law's dock when his other radio came to life, this one the Motorola two-way unit that operated on a restricted band used by the sheriff's department. It was an urgent call from Greg Hebert, the only other deputy in this north end of the parish and he was calling from nearby Henderson.

"I need to borrow your truck," Keith said; when Vic came down to ask what was going on after seeing him tying up his boat. Keith grabbed his rifle and the bag with his magazines as he explained. "Greg just called and said there was a shootout in Henderson; looters that wandered in off I-10, from what I gathered. They're pinned down in the convenience store next to A.J.'s Cafe, and he needs backup!"

"I'll drive you, let's go!"

"Better grab a rifle or shotgun then. You never know with these things!"

Keith sat on the passenger's seat of the pickup with his rifle in hand as he reflected back on all the times he'd responded to such calls since the madness began. It was unlikely that today's incident would be of much significance, because the hurricane had left so much of the area in ruins there was little left to steal and fewer people left to fight over it. Keith wasn't worried, because no matter what he encountered, nothing could top what had already happened. He would engage these thugs like all the others, and if they didn't surrender, he would kill them if he could or die trying. He was just doing his job. If not for that voice he'd heard on the radio earlier, he wouldn't care much which way it went, because until now, it seemed he had little else to lose. The final incident on the bridge had taken care of that, and the imagery of what he'd found there would be imprinted on his brain until the day he died.

Ten

THE BRIDGE WAS THE perfect kill zone—an eighteen-mile-long trap that was essentially a funnel at both ends with little hope of escape. It was the Interstate 10 crossing of the great swamp: officially called the Atchafalaya Basin Bridge, but also known locally and through it's own social media pages as the *Long-Ass Swamp Bridge*. "Long-ass bridge" was an appropriate description, to be sure. The parallel spans of concrete stretched on to the horizon, traversing a surreal and mysterious world of cypress, Spanish moss and blackwater swamp alive with cottonmouths and alligators. Once committed to the crossing, there were only two exits that presented an opportunity to get off or turn around, but just because they were there didn't mean they were easy to reach. With some 25,000 vehicles crossing the bridge on an average day before all the trouble started, traffic even then could sometimes be backed up for hours by the frequent accidents that occurred on those narrow, shoulderless lanes.

Before the latest attack, the bridge had already been the scene of a deadly incident since the riots and violence began.

That wasn't surprising really, considering it's proximity to Baton Rouge and New Orleans and the fact that I-10 was the major coast-to-coast traffic corridor across the Deep South. The first one involved a large group of ill-advised protesters who thought it would be a good idea to stand in the road as a human blockade near the midpoint, in that narrowest and most dangerous stretch where the eastbound and westbound lanes converged and crossed the main river channel. They apparently thought that impeding thousands of commercial trucks from making their deliveries would be a major victory against the capitalistic empire they despised and so desperately desired to bring down.

The clash that ensued was Keith's first taste of the growing insurrection, although he'd been following the developments in other parts of the country through the news on television and the Internet. At that time it had seemed unlikely that such problems would arise in his rural jurisdiction, although the sheriff's department in nearby East Baton Rouge Parish was certainly getting plenty of experience with both riots and terror attacks. Keith had no doubt that many of the four hundred or so protesters that got off the buses that brought them to the bridge that day were from Baton Rouge and New Orleans, reinforced by activists from other cities in the region as far away as Houston and Atlanta.

They'd seriously miscalculated in their expectations for such a campaign out here though. A rural stretch of highway in south Louisiana wasn't the same as the city streets of Berkeley or Los Angeles. Some of the protesters came armed, perhaps having some inkling of this, but they weren't prepared for drivers who refused to stop—or for truckers who stepped down out of their big rigs with their own weapons, unafraid of the consequences of using them. Keith didn't know what started the actual shooting, because by the time he and his fellow deputies got there, it was mostly over. There were bodies strewn everywhere though, amid cars and trucks with shattered glass and bullet-riddled sheet metal. The black-clad protesters that remained alive were lined up against the bridge guardrails, held at gunpoint by Levis-wearing truckers and local residents alike; all of them lacking the patience for the kind of crap they'd been seeing on the news every night for weeks.

To reach that scene in the middle of 18-miles of traffic-packed bridge, Keith and the other deputies with him had used the Kawasaki dual-sport motorcycles and small ATVs the department kept for working the mud and gravel roads at the fringes of the basin. The bikes made it possible to split lanes through the gridlock, but by the time they arrived, it was too late to intervene. Still, they'd made hundreds of arrests on both sides of the battle lines, and the incident had closed down the bridge for two days while the scene was mopped and evidence collected. The anarchists had gotten what they wanted to an extent, but many of them got a lot more than they bargained for, as they didn't live to see the results of their efforts.

At the time, it was the biggest shootout Keith had ever dealt with as a civilian law enforcement officer. He'd seen urban combat in Iraq, to be sure, but when he joined the St. Martin Parish Sheriff's Department after getting engaged to Lynn, he'd thought he was leaving all that far in the past, and the past was where it could stay, as far as Keith was concerned. He'd done his service to his country and felt it was enough. His brother Eric though, was different. Eric thrived on the adrenaline rush of combat and danger and couldn't get enough of it. Keith had looked up to him when he was younger, wanting to be just like him right up until his big brother joined the Navy and completed the intense training to become a SEAL operator. Keith didn't share his brother's enthusiasm for the water though; so becoming a SEAL did not appeal to him. He'd joined the Marines instead, hoping to serve his time on dry land, and that's what took him to Iraq. Two tours and losing three of his best friends was enough for Keith, but Eric just kept going, hiring himself out as a private security contractor after leaving the Navy. Keith rarely saw him in recent years, and had no idea where he might be now, especially since the collapse and breakdown of communications here at home. The last time he *had* seen him; Eric had been working mostly in Europe, where the kinds of things that were happening here had started even earlier. Paralyzed by sustained and constant terror attacks, several countries on that continent had unraveled into anarchy and finally, civil war. It made for lucrative opportunities for professionals of Eric's caliber, but Keith wanted no part of it. Eric's adventures had cost him his marriage, and caused him to miss out on most of his only daughter's life. Keith didn't look up to his big brother quite as much after seeing all that. How could a man give up so much at home to go and fight for strangers in places where he really had no business? Keith didn't know, but he was pretty sure Eric wasn't in it for the money alone.

Of course Keith knew that civilian law enforcement had its share of risks too, but being a deputy wasn't the same as hiring out as a mercenary, and the odds were good that he'd come home to his wife at night. He carried a gun every day, but before that first incident on the Atchafalaya Basin Bridge, Keith had fired his duty weapon only twice—once in a domestic dispute involving a drunken husband and once during a drug raid. Since then, of course, the shooting incidents were far too numerous to count, but more often they involved rifles and riot shotguns than his Glock 22. And like in Iraq, one-by-one, Keith had witnessed his close buddies fall. Law enforcement officers were targets of opportunity for the violent factions on both sides of the battle lines now, mainly because they represented authority and order in a world where those ideas became more hopeless every day.

In the beginning, the trouble was confined mostly to the cities. Keith's department was called up several times to help out with the situation in Baton Rouge, parts of which quickly became an urban war zone like much of New Orleans and most other big population centers in the region. The local authorities were overwhelmed, and the state police and even the National Guard units deployed to help were spread thin because of the scope of the problem. All available law enforcement personnel were frequently needed in the hot spots, and that included rural sheriff's department deputies, wildlife enforcement officers and even civilian volunteers. The riots had reached critical mass and as had happened in so many cities across the country, when the shooting started between the protestors and the counter-protesters, the escalation of violence exploded faster than anyone could have foreseen.

The hard-core anarchists quickly learned that such amateur tactics as blocking highways, burning cars and smashing windows would not achieve their aims. Congregating in the streets simply made them targets, and not just for the police, but for their enemies on the other side of the ideological divide as well. They still found it useful to encourage such activities among their supporters, stirring up racial issues and hatred of authority in the urban centers, but that alone wouldn't bring the change they desired. The leaders among them and the agitators funding them knew they needed to shift to the kinds of tactics other insurgents around the globe had already proven effective. Coordinated terror attacks were a good start, and it was easy enough to borrow from the playbook already in use by the Islamic jihadists who had also ramped up their activities in the U.S. amid all the confusion and chaos. The targets of choice were law enforcement officers and anyone else who represented or protected the authority of the system they loathed. Regular citizens who supported the politicians and lawmakers were fair game as well though, especially those among them who vocally opposed what the insurrectionists were doing.

Keith had no idea what the people behind all this hoped to accomplish, other than some unachievable utopian dream in which everyone who agreed with them could participate in ridding themselves of all they perceived wrong in the world. It wasn't a new concept, by any means, and Keith's father had fought against it in the jungles of Vietnam long before Eric and Keith were even born. Bart Branson had said long ago, when the two brothers were nearly old enough for military service, that the world was bound to become less stable with time, and that if they signed up, chances were good they'd see their share of war too.

"There's just too damned many people on the planet, that's the problem," their father had said. "There's no way to avoid conflicts when you've got that many people and a limited amount of land and resources. Things are going to keep shifting and the boundaries are going to change. Hell, I hardly recognize this country now compared to when I was growing up. I can't imagine what it'll be like when you boys are my age."

Keith wasn't as old as Bart had been when he used to say that, but things were indeed unimaginable now. He had hated that his father was 800 miles away in south Florida when it started, but it hadn't done any good to tell him he ought to pack up and come stay with him and Lynn for a while. Bart Branson was as stubborn as they came, and he loved what he did for a living down there, running his little boatyard on the river in a place that winter rarely touched.

Keith had talked to him often in the beginning, before things got really bad and the cell and landline networks began going down. The occasional ham radio conversations came later, when that was all they had. They'd talked some about what was going on in Keith's AO as well as in south Florida, a state that was reeling from violence as much as any in the country, especially in the bigger, more culturally diverse cities like Miami. Trouble had been brewing for years over the decisions some of those cities made to defy federal authority, and the illegal immigration issue was just one more fuse leading to the powder keg waiting to explode along racial, economic and political divides. When the burning and killing began, many such cities, including nearby New Orleans and Houston, soon found themselves in the dark. Shutting down the power grid of any major city was a simple matter due to the complexity of the systems they all relied on. The repercussions were far less predictable, however and of course the disruptions affected everyone, not just those that such actions were intended to sanction. In the end, it only gave the insurrectionists more fuel to justify their increasingly aggressive counteractions, which in turn brought even harsher repercussions—creating a vicious cycle of ever-evolving chaos and escalating violence. The tactics and scale of the attacks changed until it could no longer be considered anything less than guerrilla warfare. Keith could still remember every word of the call for backup he'd responded to after one such revenge attack that involved his own department and forever changed law enforcement operations in his rural parish.

The sheriff and three deputies, arriving in two separate vehicles, had responded to a report of a shooting on an isolated levee road in the southern section of the parish. The female caller who reported the two burning vehicles in the road with dead bodies inside them had called from a cell phone with a local area code and prefix. She'd sounded appropriately frightened and upset, according to what the dispatcher said later, but the responding officers apparently drove right into a trap laid deliberately to kill them. They did indeed find the burning cars, smashed up in the middle of the narrow, two-lane road, but when they got out of their vehicles to investigate and called back in, the reported bodies were not visible in the flames. The next transmission anyone heard from them was a desperate plea for back up. Piecing together the evidence later, it was deduced that at least three shooters opened up on them from somewhere within the woods on either side of the road, because the four lawmen were found all dead on the scene, cut down by bullets from as many different calibers.

Keith was the closest mobile unit to receive that call, and would never forget the voice of Chief Deputy Sam Trahan, urgently screaming into his handheld as already fatally wounded, he tried to crawl for the cover of his truck. Sam never made it. It took Keith nearly ten minutes to arrive, ripping down the narrow blacktop road as fast as his sheriff's department Tahoe would go. By the time he arrived, all four men, including Sheriff Landry, lay dead between their patrol vehicles and the burning cars someone had used to set up the roadblock. The officers had been stripped of their weapons, both the service pistols on their belts and the M4 carbines they probably had in hand when they got out. Keith knew even as he walked up to them that he could be next, and the hairs on the back of his neck stood on end as he scanned the wooded bottomlands alongside the road for movement, wondering from behind which tree the first bullet would come.

But whoever had done this was already long gone. Later investigation revealed ATV tire tracks in the mud a quarter mile east of the road. An old logging track that was too narrow and muddy for conventional vehicles had provided an escape route to an apparent rendezvous with a truck and trailer several miles away on the next real road. It was a planned ambush deliberately calculated to murder the first responders, who had been set up by the mysterious female caller. Losing the sheriff and three deputies in one day was a devastating blow to the department, and changed everything about the way Keith and his remaining fellow officers worked going forward. For the first time since he'd been sworn in, Lynn asked him to consider walking away from it, but quitting the department wasn't an option as far as Keith was concerned, especially not now.

"Four good men died today because they were wearing this badge," he told her. "It might be safer to take it off, but if all of us who have taken the oath to enforce the law start doing that, what's going to happen then? Somebody has to stand up and fight or it's going to be game over for everybody."

"And they are, Keith, and you can too, whether you're in uniform or not. I'm just worried because it's clear that you are a target now, just because of that badge... you and every other law enforcement officer."

That was a fact and Keith certainly understood where Lynn was coming from. The law-abiding citizens of his parish *were* doing their part, and they *were* armed, but most folks had enough to worry about just looking out for their own families. They couldn't be expected to go out looking for the troublemakers every time an incident like today's ambush happened. And they couldn't be easily organized and ordered around either. Not all of them had the same ideas about what needed doing or not doing, and most of them just wanted to be left alone, hoping they could get back to their old lives the way they were before all this started.

If the federal authorities had their way, all civilians across the country would be disarmed by now anyway. In fact, they had already mandated that and were doing their best to carry it out where they could, but it was completely unrealistic overall. Those calling for such legislation had become more vocal after every random terror attack or mass shooting for years prior, but the very fact that such incidents were increasing in frequency and number of casualties guaranteed that disarming the population would be harder than ever. By the time the massive riots broke out, most civilians were better armed than any time in history. It was far too late now to legislate firearms out of existence, and confiscation on such a massive scale wasn't going to work—certainly not now in a time of war.

That didn't stop them from trying though. Military and civilian police roadblocks were set up on major highways and interstates as well as within many cities for the purpose of searching vehicles for weapons and ammunition. It worked in many areas, as did the threat of severe penalties for those caught with them, but it would never work everywhere, and it was impossible to enforce in the rural areas, especially without the full cooperation of all local authorities. Keith and his fellow deputies had already discussed this many times with the sheriff as the violence ramped up. They had no intention of taking away the ability of their parish citizens to defend themselves, and those same armed citizens had been invaluable in keeping most of the troublemakers out of the area, at least at first.

That first incident on the Atchafalaya Basin Bridge wasn't something any lawman would want to see happen in his jurisdiction, but it was inevitable, given the tenacity of the agitators who wouldn't quit without a fight. When the bullets started flying, regular people who had never used their guns for anything other than deer hunting or target shooting suddenly found themselves engaged in a firefight. If they hadn't been armed, the outcome could have been far different. No threat of harsh penalties for keeping their firearms would convince anyone who'd survived that encounter to 'turn theirs in, and Keith certainly wasn't going to be trying to collect them. An armed citizenry was their best hope of survival now, and as things worsened in the weeks that followed, that reality was proven time after time.

The news of what happened on the bridge that day the protesters tried to block it spread far beyond St. Martin Parish, however, and eventually gave someone else an idea for the attack that came later. It had probably been planned for weeks, but executed at a most opportune moment, when the threat of the impending hurricane persuaded people to attempt a last minute evacuation, guaranteeing the bridge would be packed.

Eleven

KEITH WAS RUNNING THE river in his patrol boat that day of the attack, visiting all the out of the way communities and isolated homesteads on the back bayous that he could reach and making sure the people living there knew about the coming storm. Most folks that lived in the vicinity of the bridge, like Keith and Lynn, would ride it out in place, which was the sensible thing to do for anyone that far inland. Down in Morgan City and the lower coastal areas of the river, in St. Mary and Terrebonne Parishes, it was different. The storm surge was the danger in the tidal zones, and if the hurricane were strong enough, like an Andrew or Katrina-level event, it would be devastating for all those places that were just barely above sea level. With the men they'd lost, which included two more deputies within weeks after the sheriff was ambushed, the department was stretched thin. There wasn't a whole lot they could do in the way of hurricane preparation, besides warning those who might not know it was coming. Though it might be futile in the end, Keith was going to visit as many residents along the waterways as he could find.

"I'll try to be back before dark," he'd told Lynn. "Don't worry about me. Just stay put and stay off the roads. It's going to get crazy now that the people in the cities have figured out this thing is about to hit."

"Most of them won't have the gas to get anywhere though," Lynn said. "They'd be better off staying where they are."

"Yeah, but they won't. There'll be enough of them with just enough gas to make it to I-10 and turn it into a parking lot. All hell will break loose when the ones that aren't on empty can't move because of the ones that are. It's not anywhere you want to be, trust me."

"You don't have to worry about that. I'm not going out there, but it breaks my heart thinking about all the people who have nowhere to go to get out of the danger zone."

"I know. I wish there was a way to get them all out, but of course there isn't. And you know as well as I do that there's other kinds of danger zones elsewhere now that are as bad or worse. All I can do about the hurricane is make sure as many people know about it as possible. At least they can hunker down and try to protect their property. It's better than nothing. I'll see you later, baby. I'll try to be back by dark."

"Be safe, Keith."

He'd kissed her and promised he would, but he wasn't worried out on the river, which was much safer than any road. So far, there hadn't been any incidents on the parts of the river in his jurisdiction, which was why fuel was now being moved north by barge instead of truck or rail transport. That didn't mean it was totally safe though, and the towboat companies were certainly employing armed security, given the value of their cargo. Nothing had happened here yet though, and Keith figured that if the fuel barges did run into trouble, it would probably be on the Mississippi or its tributaries. The farther from the Gulf refineries and storage facilities they traveled, the more valuable their cargo would become. Gasoline and diesel could still be had here in the Gulf coast region, at least by those who could afford the exorbitant prices, but in places far from where it was produced; obtaining it at *any* price was virtually impossible.

It was early morning when Keith had said goodbye to Lynn, and he spent most of the day warning people along the lower reaches of the river before turning back north to scour all the smaller bayous and sloughs closer to home. It would have taken until dark at least, just as he'd told his wife, if his mission hadn't been interrupted by a call from dispatch on his secure radio as soon as he was back in range. There'd been another incident on the I-10 bridge over the swamp that afternoon. Deputy Greg Hebert had called it in, relaying what he could see of it when he got there. What he'd described sounded like a major terror attack, complete with explosions and automatic weapons. He'd called from the Butte La Rose exit near the west end of the bridge, and had no idea what it was like on the other side, but that the worst appeared to be east of the Whiskey Bay channel crossing.

Keith sped back to his house with the outboards nearly wide open. It would be faster to grab his bike and go by road, as it was a long way around to the Whiskey Bay landing and he still might need to make his way miles to the east to reach the scene. From what the dispatcher said, it might already be too late, but he was going to have to get up there anyway and find out what happened. The KLR parked under his house was the best tool he had for that, considering the gridlock he knew he'd be facing once he arrived on the bridge.

When he came around the last bend on the home bayou and cut the throttle on approach to his dock, everything looked as it had when he'd left. His white sheriff's department Tahoe, now dented and sporting bullet holes from some of his recent encounters, was parked next to Lynn's Jeep Cherokee and his old Toyota pickup. Keith had no reason to think Lynn might have gone anywhere until he tied off his lines and walked up to the house. That was when he saw something odd. The 650cc Kawasaki he intended to ride to the bridge on was there, but Lynn's smaller Suzuki dual-sport was not. It had definitely been there when he left this morning though, and it didn't make sense that it would be missing now.

"LYNN!" Keith ran up the steps to the front deck and unlocked the door. "Lynn! Where are you?"

Lynn didn't answer though and Keith only had to glance at the bar that separated the kitchen from the dining room to see that she had left him a note. He snatched it up and read the brief message. *Lynn had taken the bike!* Keith stared at her words in disbelief. She said she took it because she had to get across the bridge and figured it would be faster with all the traffic. The note explained that her sister Jeannette had called on the radio Keith had given her to tell her that their mother apparently had a heart attack that afternoon and might not make it. Jeannette and her family lived with their mother in the house Lynn and her siblings had grown up in south of Ramah, because she was nearly ninety and unable to live alone any more. Naturally, Lynn wanted to try and get there in time, regardless of the traffic jam she knew she would face on the bridge, and she'd taken the bike, knowing it was her only chance of getting across. Keith doubted Lynn knew anything about the attack when she left, and he could only hope she'd reached her destination before it started. The last thing she'd written was: *Please don't worry! I'll let you know what's going on as soon as I know. Love you, Lynn.*

Keith stuffed the note in his shirt pocket and reached for the radio microphone to try and raise Jeannette. The radios were retired base station units the department had used before their last upgrade, and after the cell phone networks went down, Keith had bought two of them and paid the technician to set them up on a secure frequency so they could communicate with Lynn's family over on the east side of the river basin. It was a reliable system, but no one answered his repeated calls, and Keith couldn't wait around to see if they would. He had to get to that bridge and hope like hell Lynn had already made it across before the attack.

Keith locked the house and rushed back downstairs to the bike. He put his M4 in the side-mounted rifle scabbard and pulled on his helmet and leather gloves. Barely giving the single-cylinder engine time to warm up, he popped the clutch and tore out down the gravel to the paved road at the end of the lane. *Why of all days, did his mother-in-law have to pick today to have a heart attack?* They all knew she'd been in poor health for a long time though, and no doubt all the stress and excitement over the approaching hurricane was a contributing factor. Keith knew that even if he'd been here, he couldn't have talked Lynn out of trying to get there before it was too late to see her, not if the bridge was still passable. He just wished she'd made a note of the exact time she'd left. From what the dispatcher said, he gathered that the attack happened about an hour before he received the call. The timing of her departure could be a matter of life or death for Lynn, regardless of whether or not her mother survived the heart attack.

Keith wound the 650 thumper to the redline as all those thoughts went through his mind. The KLR wasn't a fast bike on the open road, but it could go most anywhere, and that was more useful than speed most of the time now. When he finally came to the entrance ramp to Interstate 10, he stood on the pegs and rode around the stopped cars until he reached the eastbound lanes. Several people standing beside their cars and trucks staring towards the bridge stepped back in alarm at his sudden approach, until he flicked on the small blue L.E.D. flashers mounted on the lower forks. When he stopped and flipped up his helmet, a truck driver came over to his bike to fill him in after realizing that he was a lawman.

"It's bad," the man said, telling Keith that the details of the attack had been relayed by CB radio from other truckers caught on the bridge closer to the scene. Keith could see dark plumes of smoke in the distance, and the trucker said it was from all the burning vehicles.

"I've been stuck here nearly two hours. That's about when it started. They said a box truck blew up just past the 975 exit up ahead. Then another truck exploded on the east side of the bridge before you get to the Ramah exit. After the explosions, they said there were shooters walking through the lanes from both ends killing as many people as they could in the vehicles caught in the middle. The chatter I've heard on the radio since said it was over though. People were shooting back and I guess they finally got all the terrorists. There's no telling how long we'll be stuck. It's too backed up to turn around and who knows how many vehicles are burning on that bridge. I guess you can work your way through on that bike, but I think you're a little late to do any good, if you don't mind me saying so."

Keith thanked him and shifted into gear to ride forward, weaving between the parked vehicles or going around them on the shoulder until he reached the part of the bridge where the shoulder ended. With the blue lights flashing, and lots of beeping of his horn he managed to get people to close their doors long enough for him to slip through between the cars in the middle. The stranded drivers here were too far away to have witnessed the attack, but the news spread by the truckers over the CB had left them all in shock and disbelief. There was nothing Keith could say or do to help them now though, and despite the many that tried to stop him to ask questions, he rode on through them with his visor down.

After a little over three miles of weaving his way east, Keith was at last nearing the source of the smoke and a packed crowd of onlookers bunched together at a safe distance to watch and wait. Forcing his way through them, he passed several volunteers helping injured survivors away from the scene, and then he was there—among the bullet riddled cars and the bodies of their occupants. The carnage was horrendous beyond belief. It was impossible to fathom how anyone could do such a thing, but he'd long since accepted this as the new reality. Speaking to one of the busy volunteers he passed, Keith learned that the terrorists had used automatic weapons to do the shooting and apparently some sort of I.E.D.s to blow up the trucks. The objective was to kill as many as possible before they were taken out, and whatever the final death toll turned out to be, Keith knew it was going to be big. Whoever did this had planned it well, and it must have taken time and patience to set up, as they would have had to deal with the traffic just like their victims in order to get the explosive-filled trucks into position. Clearly the perpetrators came prepared to die, which pointed to a jihadist motive, but whether they were foreign or domestic didn't matter. Those they'd killed were dead regardless, cut down in cold blood simply because they were caught here, trying to escape an approaching storm.

The war had come here, even to St. Martin Parish, but it was a war against an enemy that hid in plain sight among civilian noncombatants. Keith didn't know how it was ever going to be stopped, but that was a question for another day. Right now he had to keep moving east, to make sure there were indeed no remaining attackers, all the while praying that Lynn had made it safely to her mother's house. When he passed the camo-clad body of one of the dead terrorists lying facedown on the concrete, he didn't even bother stopping to investigate. The bullet hole through the back of the head was a sure indication that one was no longer a threat. Keith and his fellow officers hadn't made it there in time to help stop these monsters, but armed citizens had managed to prevail anyway, once again proving that the idea of confiscating firearms in times like these was ridiculous.

On the east side of that gruesome scene, Keith came to a large group of survivors who'd been caught in the middle between the two teams from the trucks. They would be dead now too if the terrorists hadn't been stopped before they reached them. Beyond that mile-long safe zone, Keith reached the site of the easternmost explosion, along with many more bodies and burning cars and trucks. As he slowed to a stop, he saw Greg Hebert walking towards him from among a group of volunteers working on the wounded. Keith switched off the bike and removed his helmet. Greg's face was ashen as he approached. Keith waited until he was closer before he began to speak.

"I'm sorry I couldn't get here sooner, Greg. I was out of radio contact most of the afternoon. Were you here before it was finished?"

"No. By the time we got word and could get here it was over. We had to leave the truck on 975 and run on foot the whole way here. As far as we can tell there were only six tangos, three on each end. The explosions and the burning trucks gave them plenty of time though, and it could have been a lot worse if there hadn't been quite a few folks with rifles in their cars. Some of the good guys that shot back were firing from over there on the westbound span."

Keith was about to respond when Greg stopped him cold with what he said next:

"Keith, I don't know how to break it to you any easier, but we found Lynn out here too."

"Lynn? On the bridge?"

"I'm afraid so, Keith. When I saw you coming on the bike, I wondered if you two had been riding together or something before it happened, because her bike is over there...."

Keith felt as if his knees were going to buckle beneath him as he looked where Greg was pointing, back among a cluster of shot-up vehicles. He now saw the back wheel of the Suzuki, just visible where the bike was lying on the pavement on the other side of a Ford pickup. Keith was already moving towards it without conscious thought as Greg walked closely by his side. "Is she... dead?"

"I'm sorry, man." Greg put an arm around Keith's shoulder to steady him and walked with him to the place where the bike had fallen. Someone had covered the body beside it with a plastic raincoat, and Lynn's helmet, its chin strap cut away, was sitting upright on the curb at the base of the guardrail. Keith dropped to his knees next to her and lifted the edge of the coat. All she'd wanted to do was get to her mother in time to see her again. Anybody would have done the same, and like all the others who'd died here today, she had no way of knowing that she was riding into a death trap. He hadn't been there to stop her from going, and he hadn't been here beside her to defend her. Keith had never felt such a hopeless sense of failure in his life. How he would go on after this, was impossible to say.

There were wounded survivors that needed help right now though, and the storm was still coming whether all these stranded motorists got off of that bridge or not. Keith reached under the edge of his wife's shirt and removed the Glock 43 she always carried in her waistband, but hadn't even had a chance to draw today. Then he kissed her forehead and pulled the coat back over her face. The time for mourning would come later, when the work that had to come first was done.

Twelve

BURYING HIS WIFE WAS the hardest thing Keith Branson had ever had to do. They laid her in one of two fresh graves in the cemetery behind the small family church she'd attended since childhood. Between her and the decade-old grave of her father, they laid her mother, who didn't survive the heart attack she suffered that day Lynn was killed. After a somber service performed just two days after the hurricane swept through the area, Keith spent much of the next few weeks staying with his in-laws.

He'd gone back to the house he and Lynn built to check on it after the storm, but even if it weren't damaged it would have been too painful to stay there alone with all his memories so soon after her death. He secured his gear and supplies and rearranged and covered things that would get damaged by the rain until he could find the motivation to come back and replace the roof, but it was a good month before he took a real interest in it again. When it started to feel crowded at the Guidry house with Jeanette's three kids underfoot, Keith spent a few nights with his brother-in-law

Vic, but that got old too after a while and he finally resolved to go home and rebuild.

The bayou-front house was an ideal base from which to operate in the present conditions, considering its seclusion and distance from the main roads. He had everything he needed on site, and most importantly, access to the entire river basin from his backyard. He'd repaired the dock first, but that was minor compared to the damage the winds had done to the house. Large areas of the decking and metal roof panels had been torn away and scattered far and wide in the surrounding woods, taking even some of the rafters out as well. Putting it all back together would give Keith plenty to do to stay busy when he wasn't out patrolling the river.

He knew the work with his hands was good for him, keeping him from spending too much time sitting and thinking, and he knew Lynn wouldn't want him to give up the house. It had been their dream together, and the more he thought about it over time, the more he realized he couldn't just walk away from it, not anytime soon, anyway. He worked most days until it was either too dark to see or the mosquitoes were so ravenous they drove him inside to the screened-in porch. At night he sat there and listened to the night sounds of the bayou, thinking how the world beyond was quieter than it had ever been since he first laid eyes on this place.

The power was still out all over the parish and much of the region. He'd been through a couple of hurricanes since he came here, but both were years ago, when this was still a country of law and order. One of those storms had likewise left the area in the dark, but in just a matter of days, endless convoys of utility company trucks from states as far away as the Midwest and the East Coast had descended on the area to go to work. Nothing of the sort was happening now, and Keith and most everyone else he knew simply accepted the fact that they were going to have to get used to living off the grid more or less permanently.

That was certainly easier out here in the river basin than it would be in any city. Keith could cook his meals in a fire pit in the yard if he didn't want to burn propane. He could run his generator without worry that the sound would attract nearby thieves, and he could catch fish right off his dock. The hardest part of being off grid was the difficulty of communication, but they'd already been dealing with that to a lesser extent before the hurricane hit. Now, he had to run the generator to power the converted base station in the house, but he'd been using the VHF in his boat far more often anyway as he monitored traffic on the river. He'd been thinking he needed to set up a fixed VHF antenna as high above the roof as he could get it as soon as he finished with the repairs. It would give him far more range in that useful band when he was at home, and in the current situation, he wasn't worried about repercussions from the FCC for illegally operating it from a land base. When the unexpected call came in on Channel 16 from Bart, Keith could have kicked himself for not already completing that project.

Now, even as he was en route in his brother-in-law's truck to yet another situation that would likely end in a shooting, his mind was more on that call than the upcoming confrontation. Bart had to have a good reason to come here if he came all the way across the Gulf by boat. It was going to drive Keith crazy now until he found him and got all the answers. If it hadn't been for Greg's call taking him away from the river, Keith would have spent the evening running up and down the river and listening for another call.

When they arrived at the scene of the shooting, Keith saw Greg Hebert's sheriff's department pickup truck parked off to the side of the little café opposite the convenience store. Greg was standing behind the corner of the building with his shotgun in hand, and with him were two men Keith recognized as the owner of the cafe and his brother. There was another man sprawled out unmoving on the asphalt lot in front of the store, and Vic said he was pretty sure that it was the owner, an Indian fellow named Mr. Patel.

"Park over there beside Greg's truck, Vic. We'll be out of view of anyone inside that store."

The convenience store had been closed since the hurricane, of course, as had the cafe, although A.J. Greene, the owner of the latter, opened his doors every morning for a few regulars that came by to have a cup of coffee and trade whatever news they might have heard that needed sharing. Keith and Greg often dropped in themselves, and although it was way past time for the shop to be locked up for the day, Keith figured A.J. and his brother Terry must have been working on something inside when the trouble started. Greg confirmed this when Keith and Vic reached his side.

"Mr. Patel was here with A.J. and Terry when they heard glass breaking next door. He had an alarm running off a 12-volt battery system, but it wasn't turned on at the time because he was over here."

"We told him to wait for us," A.J., said, "but he took off over there in a hurry, and the next thing we heard was several gunshots. They sounded like high-powered rifle shots to me. By the time we got to the door, Mr. Patel was already dead. Whoever is inside there took a couple of shots at us too." Terry pointed to the splintered cypress trim at the corner of the cafe building."

"Your partner, Greg here just happened to come along in his truck a few minutes later and we waved him over. We've all been watching and waiting ever since."

"You don't know how many are in there then, do you?" Keith asked Greg.

"No. I still haven't gotten a look at them. They're probably holed up in the back in the coolers or store room."

"All I can tell you is that it sounded like more than one rifle to me," A.J. said.

"Are you sure they didn't slip out the back?"

"They couldn't," Greg said. "There's only one other door back there for loading and Mr. Patel had it chained and padlocked from the outside. I went around back of the café to get a look. There aren't any windows big enough to crawl out of either, just one way in and one way out, and that's the front door. I didn't really want to go in there after them without backup though."

Keith certainly understood. Whoever was in that store had already proven they had no regard for human life. What they expected to find there, he had no idea. Probably food and anything else useful, but Mr. Patel's shelves, like most every other store in the region, had long since been cleaned out. In situations like this, Keith wished he had a few grenades. They would certainly come in handy, as would a man on a M249 for backup, the way they'd done things when he was clearing houses in Fallujah. The intruders in that store deserved no quarter after killing the owner in cold blood, and Keith didn't plan to risk his life trying to take them alive.

Tear gas or flash-bangs would have been helpful if they hadn't already used up the supplies of non-lethal options they had on hand during the various riots the department had been involved in. Smoke or fire might work too, but Keith and Greg didn't really want to risk burning down the building, as it was too close to A.J.'s for that and there was always the hope that one day, somehow, stores might reopen for business in St. Martin Parish. That left them with few options at the moment other than watching and waiting. Waiting was the last thing Keith wanted to do right about now though, knowing that his father was somewhere out there in the river basin close enough that he had gotten through by VHF radio. It would be dark soon though, and wherever he was, Keith figured he would have to stop for the night. Whatever the case, their reunion would have to wait until tomorrow now. There was no way they could risk letting these killers slip out of that store in the dark, so wait it out they would.

"You might as well go back to the house, Vic," he told his brother-in-law. "Greg and I can handle this. It looks like it's just going to be a matter of waiting."

"I don't mind helping out if you need me, bro."

"I know, and I appreciate it, but they're pinned down. They're not going to hurt anyone else as long as they're inside."

"What if they don't come out? You can't wait forever, especially now with your old man coming to visit."

"No, but we'll give it 'til morning if we have to. Just do me a favor and see if you can reach him on 16 with your taller antenna. If you do, tell him I'll see him in the morning."

"What was that all about?" Greg asked, as Vic drove off into the night.

Keith filled him in on the unexpected radio call and what it likely meant.

"So, your old man came all this way from south Florida by boat? That's one hell of a trip!" Greg said.

"Yeah. I have no idea if he's running the boat or if he's just caught a ride with someone. He knows what he's doing when it comes to seamanship though. But I'm still surprised he would consider it after what he said last time I talked to him. I figure Florida's really gotten rough since then to make him change his mind about staying."

"The hurricane had to be bad there, seeing how bad it was up here. It may have been even stronger when it hit Florida that it was here."

"Maybe. Even if it weren't, the effects would be bad that far down the peninsula. There simply aren't enough roads to move that big of a population in a hurry, even if the hurricane was the only factor. With gas already unobtainable before, it must have been a nightmare. Getting out by boat would be a lot easier for those who had the option, and my father certainly did."

"Well, that's good to know. If you heard that call today, I'm sure you'll be seeing him by tomorrow. He can't be too far away."

"No, and if it weren't for these dirtbags we've got to wait out now, I'd probably be seeing him tonight."

"Sorry I had to call you man. I could have kept them pinned down by myself now that I know there's only one way out. But when I got here and saw that Mr. Patel was dead, I wasn't sure what I was dealing with and whether or not they were going to try and shoot their way out of this."

"They probably will when they get desperate enough, unless we can think of a way to get to them first."

A.J. and Terry had gone back inside the cafe building when Keith arrived. He certainly didn't want them involved, as neither of them had the training or experience for something like this. Their presence in there did give Keith an idea though.

"Maybe after we wait a bit longer, we should get A.J. and Terry to drive away in their car and your truck at the same time. If whoever is inside that store saw you drive up and saw the markings on your truck, they'll figure there was only one officer here and that he gave up on waiting."

"Hmm. That might work. What do you have in mind, one of us slipping around to the other side of the store so when they come out we'll have them in a crossfire if they don't surrender?"

"Exactly. We'll just need to make sure they don't get around to the back of that store. If they hit those woods, it'll be impossible to find them in the dark without the dogs."

"Okay, I'll go talk to A.J. and Terry. I'm sure they'll be happy to help. Don't go anywhere."

"I'll be right here watching that door. Don't worry."

They'd had a dog handler that the sheriff sometimes hired to track down fugitives in the swamps and woods, but he lived over in West Baton Rouge Parish and Keith hadn't heard from him in weeks. It didn't matter though, because he was determined that the killers in that store weren't going to make it to the woods. He'd give them one chance to surrender if they immediately dropped their weapons, but if they didn't, he would take them out, and that's what he expected to happen. It was better that way in the long run, because with the grid down, the department seriously shorthanded, and everyone doing what they had to in order to survive, dealing with prisoners was too much of a burden on available resources.

Five minutes after Greg went in to ask for their help, the two brothers came outside with him and locked the door to the café behind them. Terry drove away in A.J.'s car and A.J. took the Chevy Sierra with the department emblems on the doors, following his brother out of the parking lot and down the street to the west.

"Looks legit to me," Keith whispered. "I'll bet it will fool them."

"Yep. I told them to hide the truck somewhere and to drive back by in the car without stopping every half hour or so. That way we can flag them down if we need a ride out of here."

"Good thinking. So how do you want to do this?"

"Well, I'm up for suggestions, but if you want to stay here and cover that door with your rifle, I thought I'd slip around behind the cafe and then cut across to the east side of the store. It's plenty dark behind that corner there."

"That works for me if you're up to it. Better make it quick though. They may not wait long to make their move."

Greg was carrying his Remington 870 riot shotgun with an extended magazine. Once he was in position, he would be within 20 feet of the door and hidden in the shadows off to the side. Anyone coming out would be in point blank range for the 12-gauge, and also an easy target for Keith's M4. Keith was prone on the concrete walkway in front of the cafe so that he could just see around the corner without presenting a target to anyone inside the glass doors and windows of the convenience store. Now that it was dark, it would be hard for them to spot him there until it was too late. If they emerged before Greg was ready, he would order them to stop and he would shoot them if they didn't, but it would surely go smoother if they had time to set it up as planned.

Fifteen minutes passed and Keith suddenly saw a bright flash of light from out of the dark at the east corner of the building. It was Greg's signal, a one-second press of the momentary "on" button of his tactical flashlight, aimed so Keith couldn't miss it, but invisible to anyone inside the store from that angle. Greg was in place, but still they waited, the time seeming to drag on and on. The intruders inside the store were taking their time, and Keith wondered if A.J. and Terry might be wrong. Maybe they had found another way out and already disappeared into the woods? Or maybe they were wrong about Mr. Patel's store being all out of stock. Maybe the storeowner had hoarded a stash of food and other supplies in the stock room, and the looters were still sorting through it? Whatever it was, Keith was really getting impatient. He wanted to get this done so he could go home. He was thinking about some kind of diversion they might use to draw out their quarry when suddenly, the front door swung open without warning.

Keith watched through his compact 2.5x scope as a large figure emerged from the store, pushing the door outwards as he backed out with his arms full of stacked boxes. When he was far enough out to turn around with his load, he held the door with his foot while a smaller person carrying more boxes ducked past him. Whatever was in those boxes was obviously heavy, as the man slowly bent his knees and lowered them to the ground before letting the door swing shut again. It was at that moment that Greg's light suddenly illuminated the two thieves, causing the smaller one to suddenly stop and drop the boxes in surprise, while the other one spun towards the light and took a step back. Keith's finger was on the trigger and ready when Greg ordered the two to freeze. The looters complied and moved their hands up as they nervously looked at each other and then back at Greg, who now stepped out of the dark and in front of the store, his shotgun leveled.

It seemed that everything was under control when suddenly; there was a muzzle flash from somewhere inside the building, followed by the report of a rifle. Greg staggered and dropped his flashlight, but spun and fired a round of buckshot through the glass storefront before going down. Keith couldn't see a thing in the dark interior of the store, but he squeezed off several rounds as fast as he could fire into the area where he'd seen the muzzle flash. The two looters outside reacted by attempting to run for the corner of the building opposite Greg. Keith took aim and dropped the shorter one first, and then shot down the larger man as he drew a pistol and began firing wildly, unsure of Keith's position.

Both of the looters now lay still while Greg was crawling for the shadows at the corner of the building. Keith waited a second or two to be sure nothing was moving inside the store, and then sprinted to Greg's side, grabbing his fallen flashlight on the way. There was a lot of blood on the sidewalk, and when Keith reached him, Greg was weak and trembling.

"I'm hit pretty hard, man!"

"Where?" Keith asked, even as he was already looking for the source of the blood. It only took another second to find it. Greg's shirt was soaked and the blood was still flowing from a hole in his side, just under the rib cage. Keith held pressure on it with one hand while using the flashlight in the other to look for more damage. The wound he'd found was on the side that had been facing the shooter, and it appeared there was no exit. He had no idea what kind of round had hit him, but it had passed through the heavy plate glass storefront first, perhaps expanding and dissipating some of its energy before it struck him if it were some kind of soft or hollow-point hunting round.

"Hang in there, buddy. You're going to be all right."

Keith glanced back over his shoulder at the two dead looters on the other end of the sidewalk. If not for having to assist Greg, he would clear the store as well and make sure no one was still alive in there, but he felt pretty confident he'd taken out the unseen shooter, if Greg's buckshot blast hadn't done it first. It was quiet inside and quiet on the street out front, and Keith wished now they'd set a firm rendezvous time with A.J. and Terry to bring Greg's truck back. Keith needed to get him to someone who could help him, but that wasn't going to happen without a vehicle for transport. So now all they could do was wait, and Keith could only hope time wouldn't run out for Greg. His thoughts of getting back home tonight were forgotten now. Saving his friend's life was top priority.

"You got 'em all?" Greg asked, as he looked up at Keith. "I'd hate to die knowing any of those bastards got away."

"They didn't get away, Greg. And you're *not* going to die. As soon as A.J. and Terry get back with your truck, I'm going to drive you to the hospital in Lafayette and get you patched up. It looks like it's just a scratch to me."

"Yeah right. Couple inches higher and you wouldn't have to worry about getting me to any hospital," Greg managed, between gasps.

"Just relax and don't try to talk if it hurts. They'll be here soon."

Keith had removed his shirt and was using it as a compress on the wound. If he only had his boat or patrol vehicle, there would be a first-aid kit handy, but until the two brothers returned, he would have to make do. When he finally saw headlights coming down the road from the east, Keith watched closely from where he and Greg were hiding in the shadows until the approaching vehicle was close enough to identify. When he knew for sure it was A.J. and Terry, Keith stood and flashed the light at the driver three times; a signal that quickly brought the driver of the car to a stop.

"OVER HERE, A.J.! Greg's hit!

When the two men pulled up Keith directed them to help move Greg before he went to check the dead looters. The headlights shining through the broken glass illuminated the interior of the store enough for him to see a body sprawled on the floor there. After they had Greg in the passenger's seat, Keith made a quick sweep to collect the weapons. The dead shooter inside was a woman, as was the shorter one outside. All three appeared to be in their twenties and probably weren't criminals before the insurrection. Like so many others, they had become desperate to the point they were willing to kill an innocent storeowner just to steal some food. They'd attempted to kill his partner and friend too, and Keith didn't feel remorse for wasting them all, as he knew that Greg might die yet. He got into the car and A.J. drove them back to where they'd left Greg's truck. Once they had Greg moved into it, A.J. fished out a bottle of whiskey he had under his seat and handed it to Keith.

"This may help him a little until you get there, Keith. Good luck!"

"Thanks, A.J. I'll be stopping by to see about identifying those bodies tomorrow. I don't think there was anyone else helping them, but be careful when you go back there."

Thirteen

"DAMMIT!!!! I SHOULD HAVE opened fire on that son of a bitch!" Eric said, as he took the prop out of gear and shoved the throttle lever back to idle. This was no mere grounding on the bottom, because in a marshy place like this the natural bottom would only be mud and sand. *Dreamtime* had hit something that was as solid as a reef, and from the sound of metal grinding upon metal that he'd heard; Eric had no doubt it was something big and manmade. He helped Bart back to his feet after the impact slammed him forward against the main bulkhead hard enough to put a nasty bruise on his father's shoulder. Shauna had been thrown from her bunk as well, and her outcry of pain sent Daniel below to check on her even as Jonathan yelled from somewhere in the water where he'd been catapulted over the bow.

"How is Shauna? Is she okay?" Eric called down to Daniel.

"I think so, she just bumped her bad hand pretty hard."

"JONATHAN! Where are you, buddy?"

"I'm good, dude! WHAT THE HELL?"

Eric leaned over the rail to see Jonathan swimming beside the boat, heading aft to the stern boarding ladder. "I don't know. We hit something as solid as a rock! Can you see anything down there?"

"No, but I felt something with my foot up near the front of the boat. There's something underwater here, for sure!"

Eric leaned over the rails on both sides, looking, but could see nothing. After swinging the ladder down so Jonathan could climb back aboard, he went forward to the bow, walking on the angled port side deck—the low side now that the schooner was listing some fifteen degrees to port.

"See if you can back her off under power!" he yelled back to Bart. "I think maybe it's just the forward part of the hull that hit!"

Eric heard the engine rev to full throttle and saw the prop wash sweeping past the hull from the reverse thrust. The engine was moving a lot of water, but *Dreamtime* didn't budge from whatever she was lodged on. Eric rushed back to the cockpit and told him to shut it down, as it was apparent they weren't getting off that easily.

"Whatever it is, we're sitting on it pretty good," Bart said.

"Yeah, and the unfortunate thing about that is that we're pretty much at peak high tide. I'm going below to look for signs of damage to the inside of the hull. Then I'll go over the side and try and figure out what we're dealing with."

Down below, Eric checked the bilges and as much of the hull interior as he could access, looking for water intrusion.

"What do you think, Eric?" Shauna asked, as she sat there on her bunk with Daniel waiting for the pain of hitting her injured hand to subside.

"I don't see that it punctured the hull, so that's good. But I think we hit something big. Something big and solid and probably metal, from the sound of it."

"Something left there by the hurricane?" Daniel asked.

"Probably. It could be a wreck. I'm going to go have a look but the water is so murky it'll be more like feeling around blind than anything else."

When he was in the water with his mask, snorkel and fins, Eric swam forward along the hull to the bow, feeling the topsides as far down as he could reach along the way until he made contact with whatever it was they'd hit. Taking a deep breath, he submerged until he was on top of whatever it was, and then he eased his way along to the place where the schooner's hull was in contact with it. Just as he'd thought, it was a big metal object under there. As he swam aft again down the side of the sailboat, he was quite sure that what was under there was the hull of another vessel—a vessel that had sank and was lying on its side on the river bottom. Eric surfaced to get another breath and then dove again, exploring the perimeter of the submerged wreck to try and determine how big it was and how much of *Dreamtime's* hull was in contact with it.

Just as he'd known before he went in the water, Eric couldn't see much of anything down there, but he could feel his way along, and it didn't take long to determine that the sunken vessel they'd hit was about as long as *Dreamtime* herself, and since it seemed to be made of steel, it was probably a commercial fishing or work boat of some kind. How it ended up on the bottom here, he had no idea, but he figured it could have been an old derelict left tied up somewhere along the riverbank that got swept away in the storm surge. His guess that it was old proved correct when he discovered that part of the keel of *Dreamtime* had sliced its way right into the rusty topsides of the sunken vessel. That was far worse than if it had simply ran up on top of it. Now, with the keel wedged into that wreckage of twisted metal, getting the schooner off was sure to prove far more difficult. It was just their bad luck that such a wreck happened to be in the one spot that the inconsiderate barge captain forced them out of the channel; that and the fact that it happened at high tide too. *What a mess!*

"What do you think?" Bart asked, when Eric finally swam back around to the cockpit and pushed his mask back on his forehead.

"I think we're in quite a fix." Eric quickly told them what he'd found. "Because of the way it's jammed into that old hull, we're going to have to pull the boat straight back. If it hadn't broke through, we could probably heel her over some and slide her off, but it looks like the keel rode up onto it when it hit. There was enough momentum to cause it to ride up on it and then when enough weight was on it, the old hull just caved in. I don't know if pulling from the stern is going to work without some way to lift the bow."

"And we've got no way in hell to do that without help," Bart said.

"We won't get any from the tide, that's for sure. If this had happened on a low and there was enough range, it'd be simple enough, but no such luck for us."

"So what are we gonna do?" Jonathan asked.

"The only thing we can do is get the stern anchor set as far aft as we can and see if we can winch her back. I don't think it's likely, but we need to try it right now, because the more the tide drops the less our chance of success. I don't want to waste time untying and launching the dinghy. If you guys can pass me one of those empty Jerry cans so I can use it for floatation, I'll swim the anchor out."

Jonathan did as he was asked and handed Eric one of the empty 6-gallon plastic containers. With the cap and vent tightly sealed and the container floating on its side, it would support the big Fortress stern anchor and the thirty feet of chain at the end of the nylon rode. By hanging onto it and pushing it in front of him as he kicked with his fins, Eric was able to quickly move the anchor 200 feet aft, and then slide it off the makeshift raft and swim it to the bottom to get a good set. That done, he returned to the boat to help the crew attempt to winch her off.

They led the bitter end of the rode forward to the big windlass at the bow, as it was the most powerful winch on board and had not only a chain gypsy for the main road but also a drum to handle rope on the other side. Running it through the chocks on the stern kept the forces in line with the anchor, and when he had taken up the slack, Eric directed the rest of the crew to move as far aft as possible to try and get some weight off the bow. Everyone was crowded into the small aft cabin when he began pumping the windlass handle back and forth to reel in the line. The rode went taut and quivered like a guitar string when the natural stretch was taken up, but *Dreamtime* didn't budge even though the anchor held firm in the soft river bottom mud. There simply wasn't enough power in the manual windlass to extract the 20,000-pound vessel from the wreckage. Like Eric suspected, it was going to take a combination of lifting forces with the pulling to get the job done.

"So what do we do now, hope for a higher tide to come in?" Jonathan asked.

"We could, but we'd be waiting a long time. It would take an extra foot or more to give us the lift we need. Another storm surge would do it, but I doubt that's going to happen in the near future."

"So what are we supposed to do?" Daniel wanted to know. "We can't just stay here in the middle of nowhere."

"No, we've got to get her off, but it's going to take some help, something like a bigger boat with a boom of some kind that can give us some lift. A crane would be even better."

"Yeah, but where are you gonna find something like that now?" Jonathan asked. "I doubt any of those barge guys will be any help, especially after what that asshole did."

"Keith might know somebody. Of course we don't know if he heard the call on the radio yesterday or not. Now we won't have the reach with the masts down and no decent antenna height."

"Can't we put them back up? We'll have to, so we can try to call him," Daniel said.

"It'd be nearly impossible with the boat heeled over like it is," Bart said.

"He's right. The angle will foul up the mast raising system. Those tabernacles are designed to operate when the boat is sitting level. Winching those heavy spars up, the forces have to be coming from one direction. The higher they go up at an angle like we're on now, the more of a bind they'll be in at the tabernacles. It's the simple lever principle."

"Yep," Bart said. "We might as well forget trying that. Too much chance of damaging the rig."

"Then what do we do?" Daniel asked.

"I'm thinking someone needs to go get Keith," Eric said, looking at the inflatable dinghy that was lashed upside down on the coach roof. "We've got enough gas for the outboard to get there, right Dad?"

"I'm sure it's enough to get there, but I don't know if it's enough to get there and back."

Eric and Bart had already figured Keith's place was nearly 70 miles up the Atchafalaya from the coast by way of the river bends. They had brought gas for the outboard, but not for trips like that. The large Jerry cans had all been filled with diesel in order to have plenty of reserve for the main engine. The dinghy was only meant for service as a ship to shore tender and emergency lifeboat. But this was an emergency if there ever was one, and it seemed like a reasonable use of what gas they had for it to try and reach Keith. Their ship was solidly grounded in an exposed area of open marsh that offered no protection from storms or a possible attack. If there was any chance of saving *Dreamtime* before it was too late, Keith was their best hope. The 12-foot dinghy wasn't big enough to carry them all at any reasonable speed though, and even if it was it would be a bad idea to leave the schooner grounded and abandoned where it would be easy pickings for looters. Eric thought it best that he go alone, but Bart insisted that he shouldn't when the two of them walked forward to the bow where they could discuss their options quietly.

"I don't like the idea of splitting up at all," he said, "but in this case it can't be helped. You need an extra set of eyes and ears and somebody riding shotgun for a trip like that though. It's a long way up this river and a lot can happen on the way. Take Jonathan. I've got Daniel and Andrew to help me keep watch here."

"They might be able to help you keep watch, but that's about all. It's the same as leaving you alone here, Dad. Shauna can't help you out right now if trouble comes."

"Don't worry about me son. Just leave me that automatic rifle with the grenade launcher and I can hold my own. I doubt anyone's gonna try and mess with us anyway. Just get up there and back as fast as you can."

Eric tried to argue the point further, but Bart insisted he take the kid.

"Look, we have no idea what's been going on in Keith's jurisdiction. He and Lynn may not even be living in the house on the bayou anymore. But even if they are, they could be gone somewhere when you get there. If you turn around and leave, they may come back five minutes later and you'd never know. That's why it's a good idea to take Jonathan with you. If Keith and Lynn aren't home, but it looks like they've been living there, you may want to drop him off to wait for them while you look around the area. It's just something to think about...."

"If I knew for sure he was there, I'd take Shauna instead. Keith would know if there's a doctor anywhere nearby that could see her. That hand needs to be taken care of, or it'll never be right again. But I can't risk taking her all that way for nothing, if we don't find Keith."

"I agree. She's better off here on the boat until we know. Besides, Daniel would pitch a fit if she went off like that with you."

Eric laughed. That was certainly true. Daniel would have a hard time with that idea even if it were the best option for his wife. But Eric didn't want to have to worry about her, injured and exposed out on the river in the dinghy. If something happened to him, she would really be in a bind. He would take the kid, but he would still worry about leaving his father here in a stranded boat. Would he worry any less if Jonathan stayed behind? Eric thought about it for a minute and decided he wouldn't, although that wasn't Jonathan's fault. The kid lacked training and experience for this kind of thing, but he more than made up for it with his willingness to learn and to pitch in and do his part. Eric had been pleasantly surprised with him so far, especially in light of his initial first impressions. Jonathan had the attitude and adaptability of a survivor, and he had proven his courage under fire, a test that Eric had seen even trained soldiers fail their first time out. If they ran into trouble upriver, Eric knew Jonathan would do his best to help out. With his decision made, Eric wanted to make a plan and complete preparations without delay. If not for the risks, he would leave immediately, but he knew it was far more prudent to wait until dark, even though it would make the navigation part more difficult.

"Let's get ready Jonathan! Time for more operations training. Tonight you make your second trip upriver behind enemy lines! I want you to strip and clean that AK and make sure all the mags you used the other day are topped off. We could run into most anything up there!"

Along with the AK he had used in the open sea encounter with the two fishing boats, the kid would also carry the .357 Magnum revolver Eric had taken off of one of the two men who tried to steal his kayak in Florida. Jonathan had taken a liking to it ever since Eric gave it to him, and he'd demonstrated that he was a decent shot with it as well. Eric hoped that by waiting until nightfall, they could avoid the need to use their weapons at all, but it would be foolish to travel that far without being well prepared.

Eric also packed a few other things they might need into a couple of his smaller dry bags. He still had several of the MREs he'd brought with him in his kayak and with those and the other stores available on the schooner, it was easy to put together enough supplies to allow for contingencies. He assembled a minimal first-aid kit from the inventory he had in his gear, along with survival essentials for a stay in the woods if necessary. For navigation, he had his hand-bearing compass, binoculars and the night vision monocular that had already come in so handy here. But finding Keith's place in the maze of waterways upstream was going to be part guesswork and part reliance on Bart's memory from a visit there years prior. Eric and Jonathan sat with him in the cockpit of the schooner as Bart spread out the only Louisiana map he had, along with some notebook paper and a pencil.

"This is just a road map, but it'll have to do," he said. "It doesn't even show the bayou where the house is, but I'm pretty sure I can draw you a rough sketch."

Eric had been to Keith's place once as well, but only briefly, and only from the highway. Bart had stayed there longer when he went, and Keith had taken him fishing and given him a tour of the swamp in his boat, so he had a vague idea of the relationship of the river to the house.

"I wasn't doing the navigating, but I remember that we came out on the old river channel and went south to the big, main channel that the tow boats use to get to the Mississippi. I think you'll be able to spot the old river mouth on the west side as you head north in the channel. There are probably channel markers there, but without charts I don't know that for sure. There'll be all kinds of bayous, canals and dead lakes that you'll see leading off the river on both sides, but as long as you follow as close as you can to the levee on the west side of the basin, I think you'll find the bayou. You'll recognize his house when you see it. It's at the end of a sharp bend—at least it *was*."

That the house might *not* be there was another possibility they had considered. Keith's place was far enough inland to be safe from storm surge damage, but that didn't mean it wasn't vulnerable to hurricane winds. There was simply no way to know how bad the damage was that far inland until they went there. After what happened this morning, Eric wondered if it wouldn't have been wiser for he and Jonathan to make the entire trip in the dinghy before they even attempted to take *Dreamtime* upriver. If they could have found Keith first, he would have helped them with the navigation and given them intel on the overall situation here. The thought of doing just that had crossed Eric's mind at landfall, but he'd said nothing at the time because he knew the others wouldn't like the idea of splitting up the group. Now, they were left with no choice.

After Eric and Jonathan finished preparing their weapons and other gear, they offloaded the inflatable and mounted the 15-horse Yamaha outboard to the transom. The dinghy was a good one and quite capable of making the river trip. The Canadian couple that had owned the schooner had outfitted her well for island cruising, and hadn't skimped on the dinghy or the motor, knowing that a fast, seaworthy tender was needed in many anchorages in the islands that were situated far from the towns and villages where goods and services could be had. The one they'd chosen was an excellent rigid bottom inflatable paired with a quiet and fuel-efficient Yamaha four-stroke. It was a rig that could run upriver at a good clip without making a lot of noise. While it certainly wasn't as stealthy as Eric's Klepper kayak that was also on board and available, Eric hoped that wouldn't matter so much here. There might be more risk of being heard or spotted in the outboard-powered dinghy, but it was a risk he was willing to take. They simply didn't have the three or more days it would take to paddle that far when they didn't even know if they would find Keith at home or not. As far as Eric could tell from his underwater inspection, the schooner wasn't damaged from the grounding, but it could be if conditions changed. A storm bringing choppy waters to the river or even the wakes from more passing barges could cause the hull to move and grind against the metal of the sunken wreck. It needed to be moved free of that mess as soon as possible, and right now, finding Keith was their best hope of doing so.

The afternoon seemed to drag by, as Eric was impatient to get going. He resisted the urge to leave early though, and tried to get a couple of hours of sleep, insisting that Jonathan do the same. Sleep never came, even though he stretched out in his bunk and tried. Everyone on board was anxious, and Eric knew the rest of the crew would be dealing with an uncomfortable situation while they waited here. With the schooner firmly planted on that awkward angle, life on board was quite inconvenient. But worse than that would be the waiting and the helpless feeling of being stuck and immobile until Eric and Jonathan returned. To give them at least the option of leaving the boat in an emergency, Eric offloaded the kayak and assembled the paddles, tying it alongside the schooner before he left.

"I hope we'll be back with good news by tomorrow," Eric said, when the twilight finally faded to night and he and Jonathan were ready to depart. "If Keith isn't there, I'll spend at least a day looking for him before I give up. Without him we're back to negotiating with strangers for help, and we all know how that turned out the last time."

"We'll be right here waiting," Bart said, "unless some good Samaritan with a crane barge comes along."

Fourteen

KEITH DROVE WEST IN Greg's truck with his wounded partner, heading to Lafayette, where the only somewhat functioning hospital in the vicinity was running on generators and a greatly reduced staff. He kept south of I-10 on the small roads, still risky at night, but far less so than the interstate. It was up to Keith to get his wounded partner there, as there was no operational ambulance service to call, even if he could reach someone on the sheriff's department radio in Greg's truck. It was only a little over 20 miles, but Keith was still worried that he wouldn't make it in time. Considering where the bullet had hit and the fact that it apparently didn't exit, he wasn't sure what kind of internal organ damage and bleeding Greg might have suffered. All he knew was that it was a serious wound, and getting medical help fast was a matter of life or death.

Greg had made a tactical mistake when he placed himself in front of those glass windows. He'd assumed the two intruders that exited were the only ones in there, and it was a mistake anyone could make but it still shouldn't have happened. He and Keith didn't have headset comms like a proper entry team, but even if they had, Keith hadn't seen anything to tip him off until the woman inside fired.

Keith had put her rifle behind the seat of the truck after clearing the store. It was a bolt-action hunting rifle, chambered for .243, a common caliber used for deer hunting. There was also a Mini-14 .223 leaning against inside of the doorframe of the store, probably left there by the man who had his hands full of boxes when he and the other woman carried their loot outside. The pistol that same man had attempted to draw was a well-worn stainless steel Ruger P-90. Keith had given it and the Mini-14 to A.J. and Terry for safekeeping until he had time to come back and record the serial numbers from them. He would probably let the brothers keep the weapons if they wanted them, as he had been collecting firearms from incidents like this for so long now that he had far more than he had use for or space to store. He only kept the .243 because he figured if Greg pulled through this, he might want the gun that nearly killed him as a souvenir—or at least a reminder not to make that mistake again!

As he approached the hospital in Lafayette and drove towards the emergency room entrance, Keith flipped on the blue lights to identify himself as law enforcement to the armed security guards he knew were posted outside. The few doctors and nurses that were doing their best to help the community in this critical time were working on a voluntary basis and they had to turn many people away. Law enforcement officers were a priority though, and Greg wasn't the first wounded deputy from St. Martin Parish that had been treated there under those conditions. There were so few of them left at this point however, that Keith wondered if he might not be one of the last.

The guards quickly unlocked the emergency room doors when Keith got out and told them why he was there. One disappeared inside and in a few moments two more men came out rolling a gurney and Keith opened the passenger side door of the truck so they could move Greg inside. He was pale and shivering and obviously in a lot of pain as the men moved him. Keith followed them inside and gave a report of what happened to the nurse that greeted him after Greg was wheeled through a set of swinging double doors. All he could do after that was wait, so he found a chair in a dimly lit room off to the side and tried to make himself comfortable. As he sat there in silence, his thoughts returned to the radio call of that afternoon, and he wondered if perhaps even now, his father was at his house, having found his way off the river and into the correct bayou on his own. If so, Keith hoped he would see the tools and materials and realize repair work was being done, and that he still lived there. Surely he would also see the vehicles and the motorcycles parked there and at least wait a reasonable amount of time for him to return. As the possible scenarios played out in his mind, he had to stop himself from worrying about it. Chances were, Bart wasn't even close. It had already been mid-afternoon when he called and he was obviously too far away to receive Keith's reply at the time. They would meet up tomorrow, Keith was sure of it, but right now his friend and fellow officer was undergoing emergency surgery, and Keith wasn't leaving until he knew the outcome. He'd tried to appear positive about it in front of Greg, but they both knew this was a serious wound, as any rifle round striking the torso would be. The hours dragged by and Keith dozed in and out of sleep slumped in his chair. He was alone in the waiting room the entire time, and when the door opened again at last, snapping him awake, the man who entered was one of the doctors.

"He's in stable condition for now, but I can't give you any guarantees. There was a lot of internal bleeding. It was a hollow point bullet. We got it out but it did a lot of tissue damage and it just barely missed his spine. We're pretty limited on diagnostics right now but we think we've got all the leaks stopped inside. He'll need close observation though until we're sure, and plenty of time to recover."

"Thanks Doc. I guess there's no need for me to hang around for now then. I'll go see if I can find his daughter and let her know, and I'll be back to check on him tomorrow."

It was two hours after midnight when Keith left the hospital. There wasn't much point in going all the way to Vic's and then running his boat home in the dark only to have to return first thing in the morning, so he drove down to Greg's house in St. Martinsville instead. Greg lived alone since he was divorced, and he'd given Keith a key back when they lost so many men in the department and began operating out of their homes rather than the central office. There was a spare room there he'd used before, and Keith crawled into the bed to get a few hours of sleep before facing the busy day he had ahead of him.

Greg's wife, Brenda, had left him three or four years ago, running off to Dallas with a man she met online. His daughter, Rachel, who was already a senior in high school the year they divorced, refused to leave her friends to move away with her mother. Greg and Rachel had managed okay by themselves for a year until she moved off to college, and she'd since married her high-school boyfriend, Jimmy. The two of them lived out in the country on his parents' farm north of Lafayette, and had stayed put there when things began to break down. Jimmy's father had cattle on the land, and they were far enough off the major highways that it was unlikely the violent troublemakers would bother them. Greg had been out to check on them a few times, but Keith never went with him when he did. Without working phones of course, there was no way to get word to Rachel other than driving out there, so Keith resolved to do that first thing. He knew about where it was from hearing Greg describe it, and a search through Greg's address book on his desk gave him enough info to find it. Keith started that way around 8:30 and pulled into the driveway a little over an hour later. After filling Rachel in on the details concerning her father, and getting her assurance that she would go to the hospital to check on him as soon as possible, Keith drove back to A.J.'s Cafe to deal with the bodies at the store next door.

By the time he arrived, A.J. had notified Mr. Patel's family and his body had already been removed. Keith would write up a brief report in a notebook he found in Greg's truck, and check to see if any of the dead looters were carrying I.D. Beyond that, these incidents had become so common there was little else to be done. The bodies would be hauled away and buried without ceremony or formality, because even if they could be identified, contacting family members or anyone who happened to care would be next to impossible. After what they'd done to his partner, Keith simply didn't care who these criminals were. All that mattered was that they would never break into any more stores or shoot anyone again. He put the three Louisiana driver's licenses he found inside the notebook to bookmark the report and then went next door to tell A.J. all he knew about Greg before he left. He was anxious to get back to Vic's house and his boat, so he cut the visit short and hurried on his way. When he arrived at

Vic's, his brother-in-law was aboard his trawler, scraping rust and painting. It was the never-ending ritual of maintenance practiced by every owner of a steel work vessel.

"I tried last night and several times this morning since daybreak, but I never got a response," Vic said, when Keith asked the obvious question as soon as he stepped on board.

"Well, I guess I shouldn't be surprised. Maybe he stopped for the night somewhere close to wherever he called from yesterday. Or, there could be something wrong with his radio. It may be transmitting but not receiving, who knows? I guess I'll run back to the house on the chance he's already there."

Keith left Greg's truck parked at Vic's and headed south in his boat. He didn't pass any other vessels in the short run along the old river channel down to the bayou cutoff, and when he arrived at his dock, he found it just as he'd left it the day before. Keith tied up and went inside to make himself something for lunch, and ate it while sitting and staring at the gaping hole that still let in daylight through the roof. He hated to miss a day of perfect working weather with so much left to do, but he knew he couldn't focus on it anyway knowing his father was somewhere nearby. The work could wait. He wanted to make a loop over to the Whiskey Bay Pilot Channel and run it north of the bridge to see if he might spot whatever vessel Bart was on over there. He also planned to go back to the hospital and check on Greg again later that afternoon or evening. Knowing it could be days before he actually got back to work on his roof, Keith secured the big blue tarp he'd been using over the section that was still open to the weather and then collapsed his extension ladder and laid it on the ground next to his saw horses.

When he was back in his boat he tried the radio again, of course, even though by now his expectations of getting through to Bart were quite low. When he reached the river, he made the five-mile run down to the junction with the Whiskey Bay Pilot Channel, stopping for a few minutes when he got there to try the radio again. Not long after he turned north, he overtook a tow pushing several barges but still saw no vessels that his father might have called from. Keith was beginning to wonder if he was losing his mind, and if he had not imagined the calls from the day before. He'd been through a lot lately, losing Lynn and so many of his friends and fellow lawmen, but a call from his father here was so unexpected that it simply *had* to be real. It was simply so unlikely and unexpected he knew he wouldn't have dreamed it. No, Bart had really called, but he must have been farther away than Keith originally thought. The VHF band was typically used for relatively close-range communications, but with the right antenna and enough transmitter power, Keith knew it was possible to reach out farther. If Bart had a chance to do so, Keith knew he had the knowledge to set up such a system on any vessel he might have left the boatyard on. It was just surprising there had been no more calls since yesterday, though. Keith would have thought they'd be more frequent the closer he got, if he were indeed on his way.

He ran the channel north for 15 miles until he passed under the I-10 overpass and then continued on to the north end of the old river split and headed back south to return to Vic's place. By the time he was back in Greg's truck and driving to the hospital again it was already getting dark. One of the security guards at the emergency room doors recognized him from the evening before: "You brought the wounded officer in last night, right? The one you said was your partner?"

Keith froze at the question, fearing the guard was about to give him bad news. "Yeah, that's right. Do you know his status?"

"His daughter was here all afternoon. You just missed her, in fact. She asked if you had been back. She said her father was asking about you, and that he told her you saved his life."

Keith felt a flood of relief as he thanked the guard and made his way inside the hospital. A nurse directed him to the room and he found Greg asleep when he got there, no doubt sedated with pain meds, but alive and in recovery. Keith plopped into the chair in the corner of the room, thinking he would just sit there a few minutes while he thought about his plans for tomorrow. But he was a lot more exhausted than he realized after being awake most of the night before and then running back and forth all day. He fell asleep in the chair and if any nurses or doctors came in the room to check on Greg, they didn't bother him, because when he finally woke up and looked at the clock, it was nearly 4 a.m. It wasn't what he'd planned to do, but he needed the sleep and it didn't really matter where. Now he wouldn't have to wait long for daylight, and then he would drive back to Vic's and get his boat. If there was still no sign of Bart at his house, Keith thought he would head south on the river towards Morgan City today to have a look down there. He was just about to leave the room when Greg woke up and saw that he had a visitor.

"How are you feeling, man? The doctor said you'd be in some pain, but I guess they've been keeping you pretty medicated."

"Yeah, I'm more groggy than anything else. I guess I got lucky, didn't I? It could have been worse."

"A lot worse! A .243 in the torso is no joke. The doctor said it just missed your spine by millimeters."

"Good thing I had you there for backup so they didn't shoot me again. Thanks for going out there to tell Rachel, too man. I really appreciate it."

"Of course. The security guys said she told them she was coming back today. I may not make it back myself until tomorrow. I still haven't been able to get in touch with my father since I received that radio call, so I'm going to spend the day looking for him. Probably run the river all the way down if I have too. I'll get back to check on you as soon as I can. Don't worry about your house or anything. I went by there last night and everything is fine."

"I wish I could go with you and help you look for him."

"Yeah, I know. Don't worry about it though. You've got some healing to do, so get after it. I'll see you soon."

By the time he drove back to Vic's house from the hospital, it was less than an hour until daylight, and Keith knew Vic would already be up with coffee brewed. He went inside to have a cup and Vic told him he'd tried radioing his father again to no avail.

"It does seem kind of strange that he was close enough to get through to you the day before yesterday and yet he's still not here. He's either not receiving or he somehow made the call from a long way off."

"Yeah, that's what I'm thinking. I'm going to run back up the bayou one more time and make sure he's not there, and then I'm going to make a run downriver, at least to Morgan City... maybe on to the coast. You wanna ride with me?"

"I'd love to, bro, but I promised my Aunt Francine the other day that I would go over there this weekend and help them with their roof. She's going to be expecting me."

"I didn't even realize it was Saturday already," Keith said, "there's so much going on."

The truth was that the days had all been more or less the same to Keith since Lynn died. Besides that, with no one working a regular schedule anymore and most stores and businesses shut down and communications offline, the days of the week were of little importance to most people. Keith just got up everyday and did what he had to do; never knowing what that would be until it was time to do it, like when he'd gotten Greg's call for backup. Today his schedule was wide open as of now, and going downriver to look for his father was as good a use of his time as anything else he could think of. The first hint of dawn was beginning to lighten the sky, and he was ready to get going.

"Be careful on the road," he told Vic, knowing that his brother-in-law was fully aware of the dangers out there and that he wouldn't go anywhere unprepared and unarmed.

"Oh I will. I'm leaving later this morning and I'll be coming back well before noon tomorrow. Good luck on the river today, bro."

Keith carried a cup of Vic's coffee out to the boat with him and started the twin outboards as soon as he stepped aboard. While they were warming up, he got on the VHF radio again, of course, but after repeating his transmission three times and getting nothing, he hung up the mic and headed to the bayou for home. He had no expectations as he turned the final sharp bend in the winding bayou and came into view of his house. He hadn't seen another soul since he'd left Vic's dock, and when he pulled up to the pilings of his own, everything looked just as he'd left it until he stepped out of the boat to finish tying off his lines. That was when he noticed that his sheriff's department truck was missing. Keith had already slung his M4 over one shoulder when he left the boat. Now he quickly brought it to ready and then shouldered it when a man suddenly walked into view in the gravel drive that led to the road out front. The man was headed towards the house but apparently hadn't spotted Keith yet in the dim light of dawn. He would give this stranger only one chance to comply before he opened fire. Whatever he was up to, Keith stopped him short with his command: "YOU THERE! FREEZE! KEEP YOUR HANDS UP AND GET DOWN TO YOUR KNEES! NOW!"

Fifteen

ERIC AND JONATHAN QUIETLY motored away from *Dreamtime*, heading upriver into the night. There was enough ambient light out on the broad river channel to see the way though, surrounded as it was on all sides by open marsh. Eric sat in the stern at the tiller of the outboard, keeping the dinghy in the middle of the river as Jonathan scanned ahead for danger with the night vision monocular. Bart had doubted they would see signs of life on the river at night south of Morgan City, and he was right. The marsh here was mostly uninhabited even before the hurricane, and oil field activity had ceased in the aftermath. Barges like the one that had forced them out of the channel probably weren't running at night either, since they could no longer use GPS to aid in their navigation.

Eric still couldn't figure out why that captain had behaved so aggressively towards their schooner. He had plenty of room to pass without coming that close, but he'd used every bit of the channel on their side of the river. Was it just out of spite, or were the barge captains taking the offensive position around all smaller vessels because of the danger of attack? Thinking about it made Eric wonder if he really wanted to get involved with those guys, trading security services for a ride upriver. Of course they probably weren't all the same, and maybe that particular captain was simply having a bad day. Eric knew he probably made a mistake giving up the channel so readily. The captain may have been simply messing with them and might not have followed through with actually running them down, but watching him bearing down, Eric hadn't trusted he could turn in time to miss them even if he wanted to. Besides, he'd expected there was a bit of elbowroom outside of the channel anyway, as there often was in most places. The schooner only drew four feet, so there wouldn't have been an issue if not for that damned wreck they couldn't see. The grounding was a serious enough problem, but hitting something solid like that at full speed could have ended far worse. If the hull had been breached, they would *all* be in the dinghy now, towing the kayak and as many of their supplies as they could carry away. The Colvin schooner was apparently built as well as Bart said it was though, and from a very strong alloy too. It was the perfect vessel for what Eric had in mind later, after he had Megan, and he intended to do everything in his power to get it free and dock it somewhere reasonably safe while he went to find her. Without *Dreamtime* and the means to sail someplace far away, they would be little better off than everyone else here.

Things were sure to get worse long before they got better, and the survivors left with limited options were going to get a lot more desperate and dangerous. Eric felt far better about taking his chances at sea. He'd had enough of fighting hopeless battles to change things that probably couldn't be changed.

He was confident that the boat could be saved if they acted quickly. If they couldn't find Keith, he would find someone else who could help them. He'd come prepared for that as well, as they were traveling a long way up river and he didn't intend to go back until he'd arranged a solution. The weight of the small pouch of Krugerrands in his pocket reminded him how fortunate he was to have the means to pay for such help if it came to that. Gold would always work to get things done, no matter how bad the economic situation got, and Eric had enough to get a *lot* done.

He kept the dinghy at just enough speed to plane, a pace that would be fuel efficient and still relatively quiet from far away. When they reached the area of Morgan City, scattered lights powered by generators and open fires here and there shone against the backdrop of damaged buildings and houses. There were barges and various workboats and fishing vessels docked along the waterfront, but even in the dark, Eric could tell that there was barely any activity here despite how busy this place had once been. Morgan City was situated in the center of a junction of waterways, including the route to the

Gulf from which they arrived. The Gulf ICW connected the river to Texas as well as to points east, and the Atchafalaya and some of its smaller bayous converged near there from the north. Their route north would be on that main river channel, which flowed down the western side of the basin, but to get there they had to wind through Morgan City's hurricane-devastated industrial waterfront. As they passed beneath the low bridges Bart had been concerned about here, Eric kept to the middle of the channel to keep some distance from the banks in case someone happened to spot them. Jonathan kept a continuous lookout for movement, switching between night vision and the regular binoculars, but if anyone was watching them motor by, he didn't see them.

"This is pretty messed-up, dude," Jonathan said, over the hum of the Yamaha. "It's worse than anything we saw in Florida. That hurricane must have been a badass storm when it came through here!"

"I'm sure it was. You saw what was between here and the Gulf—not much of anything. They would have gotten the full force of it here. Most of the people that lived here are probably dead or have moved on."

Regardless of the greatly diminished current population, Eric felt too exposed out there on the river, even in the dark of night. It was a relief when the last of the lights disappeared behind them as they moved north. It was hard to discern much of the landscape in the dark, but Eric could see that the riverbanks here were wooded. Bart had said that north of Morgan City they would be entering the main Atchafalaya Basin. The vast expanse between the levees was said to be the largest swamp in North America and much of it was heavy river bottom forest subject to seasonal flooding. Eric knew such a place would make a good hideout for insurgents. With the country in chaos as it was, and various factions fighting against the government as well as each other, many of them would be claiming territory from which to base their operations. He had no idea if any such groups existed in these parts, and he had no desire to find out. He had no time for that kind of fun and games now, and hoped he never did again.

The main river channel of this part of the river was still wide enough that it was easy to follow in the dark. They passed several junctions with other waterways entering the river from the west, like the one they were looking for, but all of them were too far south based on Eric's dead reckoning calculations, so he passed them without even slowing. There were floating channel marker buoys in the river too, but other than to confirm they were on the main route, they meant little to Eric without the charts necessary to identify them. His estimate was that they would be in the vicinity of their turn-off when they had traveled for approximately three hours after leaving Morgan City. The Yamaha purred along flawlessly, making it easy to maintain a constant speed, and when they were close, Eric favored the west side of the river so that they wouldn't miss the junction.

"That's got to be it," he said, aiming the bow of the inflatable towards the wide opening of another channel angling in from just west of due north. "It's in the right place and coming in from the right direction."

"So we go up that channel a few miles, and then we'll be looking for a bayou cutting off to the left?" Jonathan asked, when Eric slowed down for the junction.

"Yep. Dad said it's the first one that we'll come to and that we can't miss it."

"This place is awesome!" Jonathan said, as he stared into the dark and mysterious stands of tall cypress trees that grew right to the edges of the old river. Many of them had been damaged by the storm, but the forest was still impressive. "I'll bet your dad is right about the fishing here, and there's nobody around. This is way better than Florida!"

"Don't speak too soon. We won't really know what's going on until we talk to Keith. Let's just hope *he's* still around."

Eric steered them up the smaller, old river channel at a much slower pace than he'd run the big river. There were logs and big drifts of storm debris caught in the eddies near some of the bends, and he was leery of hitting something in the dinghy after what had already happened to the schooner. The RIB was much tougher than an ordinary inflatable, but it would still be possible to rip open the tubes if they hit a sharp object at speed. In just a few miles, they came to the mouth of a large bayou branching off the river to the southwest, just about where Eric expected it would be.

"This has got to be it. Everything about it looks right."

"So, we just follow this bayou until we see the house?"

"Yep. Unless someone else has built there since, it'll be the first one we come to. Keith's place is the only one this far down."

Eric had been impressed that one time he'd visited Keith and Lynn at their bayou home. Keith had been lucky to find a piece of property like that—isolated from nearby neighbors, yet still accessible both by water and the small paved road that paralleled part of the bayou. They both seemed to love it there. It was similar to the kind of place where Lynn grew up on the east side of the basin, and ideal for Keith as it was in the jurisdiction of St. Martin Parish and relatively close to the sheriff's office in St. Martinsville, despite how remote it seemed surrounded by the enclosing woods.

Eric took it even slower on the bayou, steering clear of the protruding branches of downed trees that had fallen in from the banks. Unless Keith was out working tonight, Eric figured he would be at home and likely asleep at this hour. He didn't want to alarm him, and more importantly, didn't want to get shot. He and Jonathan had already come close to that when they'd approached his father's boatyard on the

Caloosahatchee in the wee hours of the morning. Keith was every bit as dangerous as their old man, and with what he'd probably been dealing with here as a sheriff's deputy, he would likely take no chances with intruders. Eric had brought his handheld VHF radio with him, and now that he knew he was close to Keith's house, he slowed to a stop and tried calling him with the transmitter on the low-power setting. If he had a radio in his patrol boat, it might be on. He probably wouldn't hear it from inside the house, especially if he was asleep, but Eric thought it was worth a try, even though the result was as he expected.

"We'll just have to yell when we get within sight of the house. Maybe he won't start shooting if he hears his name."

"That's really reassuring, dude."

"Yeah, well it's all I got right now, so we'll take our chances."

When they rounded a sharp bend, Eric was surprised to see that they were closer to Keith's than he'd guessed. The house was there on the west bank dead ahead, elevated fully ten feet above ground level on heavy wooden pilings. New metal roof panels reflected the moonlight from one corner, but part of the roof was covered by what looked to be a tarp, probably because of hurricane damage. There was a low dock along the waterfront adjacent to the house, but no boats were tied up there. Eric knew that didn't mean anything. Keith could have lost his patrol boat to the hurricane or someone else in the department might be using it. He was certain this was the right house though, because it was just as he remembered it from his one visit. There was no generator noise and no lights shining inside the house or out. Eric eased the dinghy closer and scanned the property with the night vision monocular. The best indication that someone might be at home was the presence of three vehicles parked out front. One was a white SUV with a sheriff's department emblem on the door. There was also a silver Jeep Cherokee and the old blue Toyota four-wheel-drive pickup that Keith had owned since before he joined the Marines. In the open space under the house, Eric saw two motorcycles chained to one of the pilings and a couple of mountain bikes hanging on a rack. He stood in the dinghy and yelled his brother's name and waited, watching the windows for signs of movement or a light. But there was nothing. It seemed no one was at home, despite all the vehicles at the house. Eric figured Keith was gone in the boat, probably out working tonight. *Maybe Lynn was staying somewhere else, with her family perhaps?* It made sense that Keith wouldn't leave her out here alone considering what was happening everywhere.

"What do you think, man? I guess he's not here, huh?"

"Probably not, but maybe he's nearby. Let's pull up over there where the dinghy is out of sight and go have a look around."

"Why not just tie up to the dock dude? That's what it's for."

"Because we don't know who might come down that bayou, that's why. Better we see them before they see us. The dinghy will be out of sight in those cattails over there. It's just a precaution."

"Duh, I guess I'm pretty stupid."

"Everybody's got to learn somehow. You're doing fine, Jonathan."

When they were ashore, Eric cautioned Jonathan once again, telling him to bring his weapon but to stay put at the water's edge until he checked for trip wires and other security measures his brother might have implemented. He immediately spotted a couple of small cameras mounted in inconspicuous locations under the cornices, and figured there were probably more of them hidden around the property. Keith would be able to run them off batteries and use the recording capabilities, but with no Internet connectivity, they would be useless for remote monitoring. He didn't really expect to run into Claymores or anything like that, but he knew he could never be too careful because he had no idea what his brother had been up against here. When he was sure it safe to proceed, he waved Jonathan forward while he checked the vehicles.

The sheriff's department SUV was sporting several bullet holes in the side panels and one through the rear window glass. There were deep scrapes and dents in the bodywork as well; clearly indicating Keith had been dealing with some trouble here. He looked into the interior with his weapon light, and saw that there was a two-way radio mounted under the dash, as he expected. Maybe he could use it to reach Keith in his boat. It would be his next step, after he checked the house. A closer look at the old Toyota truck revealed that it was sitting on jack stands under the front axle, the drive shaft disconnected and the transmission pulled. Looking into the Cherokee that he assumed was Lynn's car, he saw that it had a steering lock on the wheel.

Eric told Jonathan to wait and keep a lookout while he went up the steps leading to the house to have a look in the windows. The screen porch door had no latch, so Eric opened it and went in, calling loudly for Keith again just in case, before rapping hard on the front door. No one was home, he was sure of that now, so he shined his high-intensity Surefire weapon light through the window to look inside. A sweep of the small dining room revealed something on the buffet table against one wall that stopped him cold. More than a dozen framed pictures of Lynn were carefully arranged around a collection of candles and a vase of wilted flowers. A thick book that appeared to be a photo album was laying flat on the table, with what looked like a hand-written letter placed on top of it. Eric didn't have to guess that what he was looking at was a shrine. Something had happened to

Lynn since the last time Keith had spoken with their father. Seeing this, Eric wondered if Keith was even living here anymore, but he'd obviously put that shrine together, and Eric noticed sawhorses and lumber in the backyard and a folded extension ladder on the ground next to them. Keith or someone had been making repairs since the hurricane, but that didn't mean he was spending the nights here, it didn't mean he'd be back tomorrow, either. Eric couldn't afford to waste a lot of time waiting for nothing. Every minute that he left Bart and the others stranded down there in the marsh, they were at risk. He descended the steps to tell Jonathan what he'd discovered.

"I'm going to see if I can reach him on that radio in his patrol truck first. If not, I'm going to go find the sheriff's office. If anyone is there, maybe they'll know where Keith is. He may even be spending the nights there, for all I know. If he is, it'll be worth it to go there and find him so we can get going sooner. But you need to stay here and wait, just in case Keith happens to come back while I'm gone. We don't want to miss him so we can't both go."

"That's fine with me man, but what are you going to do, break out the window in his truck? Even if you can get in there to use the radio, you'll still have to hotwire it to drive it anywhere, won't you? You might get shot if you're seen driving a stolen sheriff's department truck."

"I'm not stealing it. Keith's my brother, man. He won't mind if I borrow it. Besides, I don't think I'll need to break in or hotwire it. I'll just use the key."

"You found the key?"

"No, but I know where it is. I'll bet there's one for each of these vehicles in the same place. Come on, I'll show you."

Eric crawled under the rear of the SUV and felt around until his fingers ran over a small lump on the bundle of wiring leading to the trailer light connection. He unwound the electrical tape from it and crawled back out with a key in his hand. Bart had been in the habit of hiding spare keys under his vehicles long before those little hideaway magnetic boxes came on the market. Eric and Keith did the same as soon as they were old enough to drive, because Bart wasn't coming to rescue them if they were careless enough to lose a key or lock one up inside a vehicle. The lesson had stuck for Eric, and he'd guessed right that it did for Keith too.

"It's a wonder someone else didn't find it and steal it already," Jonathan said.

"Nah, it isn't obvious unless you know what to look for."

Eric opened the door and slid into the seat so he could reach the police band radio control head. He turned the switch and tried adjusting the volume and squelch, but the radio was dead. Thinking maybe it required the vehicle auxiliary power to work, Eric turned the ignition key but still got nothing. "So much for that idea. It couldn't be that easy, could it? I'm going to see if I can find that sheriff's office. You keep a sharp lookout while you're waiting for me. Watch the road and the bayou. If Keith shows up, tell him I'll be right back."

Eric unslung his M4 and put it and spare mags for it on the seat beside him. When he left Keith's gravel driveway, he turned north onto the narrow paved road that paralleled the bayou, guessing it would take him to an intersection where he could turn west in the direction of town. He'd been there with Keith that one time he came to visit, and it wasn't like St. Martinsville was a big city. He passed a deserted cafe and convenience store after he made his turn, and soon spotted a sign indicating St. Martinsville to the south at the next junction. There was also a sign pointing to Interstate 10 to the north, and Keith wondered if major highways like that were still in use here or mostly abandoned as he'd heard so many of them were in Florida. There was no one traveling on the smaller roads he was following, but then again, it *was* 0300. Like most of the other towns and cities he'd passed through since arriving back in the States, there were few signs of life here at night. City streetlights, storefronts, billboards and everything else of the sort were blacked out. If people were at home in the houses he passed, they were asleep or keeping a low profile. Even in the dark, Eric could see considerable evidence of hurricane damage. Much of the debris had been pushed out of the streets, but the piles hadn't been loaded up and hauled away. Like south Florida, the grid was down indefinitely and the people who remained here were getting by without it. He found the sheriff's office building after driving around several blocks in the main part of town. Much to his dismay though, there was no sign that Keith or anyone else was working there. The front doors had been boarded up with heavy plywood, and there were no patrol vehicles parked outside. Keith pulled up as close as he could get to the main entrance and got out to look around. Upon closer inspection, he saw dozens of bullet holes in the plywood panels over the doors. What that indicated, he wasn't sure, but the building certainly wasn't in use and hadn't been for a while. He wondered if the sheriff's department had relocated their operations elsewhere, but there was no one around to ask.

While driving around looking for the building, he'd noticed a large bayou just a block and a half to the east. Eric got back in the truck and drove over there, looking up and down the banks for any sign of a patrol boat. There were houses on the opposite shore with small docks, but he didn't see any boats at any of them. Wherever Keith was, it was unlikely that he was working from here. Eric hated to do it, but he resigned himself to going back to his brother's house to wait. Driving around out here in the dark with no real idea of where to look was just a waste of time, not to mention an unnecessary risk, as he soon discovered.

He had retraced his way north to the road that paralleled the interstate and was driving towards Keith's road when he came around a curve and saw two vehicles blocking the narrow lanes. Both of them had been heading the same way Eric was traveling, but they were now stopped alongside each other. The one in his lane was a small crossover-type hatchback car. The other one sitting to the left of it was a full-sized pickup truck.

There were people outside at the rear of the truck, and Eric had come upon them so quickly when he rounded the bend that they were caught by surprise in his headlights. Everything happened fast after that point, but he'd seen enough to get an idea of what was going on. Eric wasn't here to help strangers, but the girl or young woman that was struggling and trying to fight back as two men forced her into the bed of the pickup made him instantly think of Megan. Besides that, these people were in his way. He would either have to drive around them on the shoulder or turn around and try to find another road to take him back to Keith's. Seeing him come to a stop, one of the men had already let go of the girl to move towards the cab of the pickup, probably to grab a weapon. Eric figured he would get shot at no matter what he did, so he flipped his lights on high beam and then quickly searched the console of the Tahoe until he found the switch that activated the blinding, high-intensity blue police lights. Using the lights as a diversion and keeping low, Eric exited the vehicle just seconds before a shotgun blast shattered the windshield.

Sixteen

THE MAN IN HIS driveway stopped immediately at Keith's command, putting his hands up in the air and dropping to his knees as ordered without hesitation. Keith had centered his riflescope on the stranger's chest at first, but now moved the reticle to his cheeks. The intruder looked young—despite the thin beard that shadowed his face. Keith could now see that he had a rifle slung over his back and a large revolver in a holster on his belt. He had every right to go ahead and pull the trigger. This guy was trespassing on his property at a time when people were regularly murdered in their homes. Since his patrol truck was missing too, it was likely this guy was connected to that, his accomplice already gone while he came back to steal one of the other vehicles or break into the house. But Keith wouldn't shoot him unless he had to, at least not before he got some answers. Watching him carefully for any signs of non-compliance, he slowly stepped forward into easier speaking range.

"I want you face-down on the ground with your arms straight out to the sides!" Keith yelled again. The stranger hesitated longer than he liked this time. "DO IT NOW, OR DIE NOW! YOUR CHOICE!"

"WAIT! Don't shoot! You're Keith Branson, aren't you? The deputy sheriff that lives here?"

Keith paused, surprised to hear his name, but kept the rifle trained on the stranger's chest as he answered.

"Maybe. Who's asking?"

"My name's Jonathan. I'm here with your brother, Eric! We came here to find you, man!"

Keith was really confused now as the stranger's words sank in. *Eric? How could his brother Eric possibly be here now?* He started forward again, still cautious.

"Don't move!" he warned, as he quickly closed the gap, keeping the rifle on the stranger despite what he'd just said. "What do you mean, you're with my brother, Eric? How do you know Eric?"

"I met him in Florida, man! He stopped near my campsite in the middle of the night when he first sneaked ashore in his kayak. We ended up hanging out a while and then he invited me to come along as crew when he sailed here."

"Eric Branson? My brother? Look, I don't know how you know his name, but you're full of shit. Eric is somewhere in Europe. I haven't talked to him in nearly six months."

"No, dude! I'm not bullshitting you. He's *here!* Or at least he was until just a few hours ago. We came up here to find you because the schooner got stuck in the river down near the coast. Bart and Shauna and Daniel and Andrew are still on board it, waiting on us to get help."

Keith lowered his rifle upon hearing this and walked directly to the kneeling man, still reeling in disbelief as he tried to process all that he heard. But as soon as he heard the man say his father's name, he knew it was true. Now the mystery of his father's radio call was about to be solved.

"Schooner? What schooner?"

"It's a Colvin schooner, man. It's named *Dreamtime*, but that's not the real name. Bart and Eric renamed it before we left the boatyard."

"You sailed with them from my father's boatyard, on the Caloosahatchee?"

"Yep, that's the one. All the way across the Gulf. We were gonna motor up the river right here to your place but that freakin' barge captain ran us out of the channel and we hit an old wrecked boat sunk by the hurricane. The schooner is stuck good, man! Eric said it's going to take a crane or something to get it off. That's why we came up here to find you. Bart figured you would know somebody."

"How did you get here then? And where is Eric now? Where is my truck?"

"We came in the dinghy. It's over there in those weeds," he pointed to the patch of tall cattails growing at the edge of the bayou just upstream from Keith's dock. Keith hadn't even glanced that way when he arrived and stepped off his boat, but it was conceivable that a small boat could be hidden there. "Eric didn't know who might come along, so he didn't want to leave the dinghy out in the open, tied to your dock. He hid it like he always does. He's an expert at that shit, you know. Can I put my hands down now?"

Keith was now standing just a few feet away. There was no reason to doubt this guy anymore after all he said. He had to be telling the truth to know even half of what he'd just told him. "Yeah, sure. I'm sorry, but the way things are these days, you can never be too careful." Keith stepped forward and extended his hand. "What did you say your name was?"

"It's Jonathan. Jonathan Coleman."

They shook hands when the young man got to his feet. Keith saw that he was lean and tan from outdoor living, and that the weapon he wore on a sling was some kind of AK-variant rifle.

"I'm still confused about how my brother Eric fits into all this," he said. "I got a VHF radio call the day before yesterday, late in the afternoon, from my father, so I already knew he'd somehow made it here to Louisiana on a boat. But I never could get back in touch with him and I couldn't find the boat he might have called from. I suspected he might have been farther away than I first thought, and what you said confirms it. *But Eric?* I never expected *Eric* to be with him."

"He came back here to get Megan," Jonathan said. "I met him the first night he was back, after he paddled ashore near Jupiter. He went to Shauna's house first and found it looted and deserted. Then, he and I sailed a little 25-foot boat all the way down around the Keys and up to Fort Myers. They had a blockade at the mouth of the river there, so we had to ditch the boat. We used Eric's kayak to sneak around it and go to your dad's boatyard, and that's when we found out Shauna and Daniel and Andrew where there. But Shauna hadn't seen Megan since all the riots and shit started. She said as far as she knew, Megan was still in Colorado at the university. Eric's going to get her, and when he finds her, he's planning on sailing away from all this crap. Going anywhere in Florida on the roads is about impossible anyway, and your dad thought Eric ought to come here first. He said he might want to think about hitching a ride upriver part of the way by working security on a fuel barge, because it sure as hell won't be easy to get to Colorado by road with the way things are."

Keith was flabbergasted to hear all this. He hadn't expected Eric to be able to make it back to the U.S. from Europe even if he wanted to, and until now he wasn't sure his brother *had* wanted to. But he'd somehow gotten to Florida and then sailed here from across the Gulf, bringing not only their father, but also his ex-wife and her family. Keith never would have dreamed it.

"So where is he? Why isn't he here with you if you two came here to find me? Did he take my truck?"

"Yeah, he found the key and said he was going to look for the sheriff's office and see if they might know where you were. He figured you'd been here some, since we could tell someone was working on the house, but he said you might not be living here anymore. He looked around a bit and shined his light through the windows. He saw the pictures inside and thought something might have happened to your wife."

"Yes, she died."

"I'm sorry to hear that man, I really am. And I know Eric was upset about it too. He's been gone I don't know, maybe three or four hours? We got here just before midnight and he couldn't stand just waiting for daylight, so he left. I got bored waiting on him so I walked up the road a bit. I came back when I heard your boat motor. That's why I was out here in the driveway when you first saw me. I guess I should have yelled first, but I wasn't sure it was you. Eric said to be careful, because anyone could come along out here. I'm glad you didn't shoot me, man."

"Yeah, me too, Jonathan, because I wouldn't have known who in the hell you were if I had. With all the looting that's been going on though, a lot of folks would have shot first without saying a word. I guess my law enforcement training is still too engrained in me to get used to that idea yet. Still got that bring 'em in alive for a fair trial and all that, mentality, you know? Come on, let's go up to the house and talk while we wait for Eric to get back."

As they sat on the screen porch, Jonathan answered Keith's many questions about their voyage from Florida and the specifics of the predicament the sailboat was in now. Keith immediately thought of Vic and his outrigger-equipped trawler. It might be possible to do the job with his boat alone, Keith's patrol boat with it's twin 150s could provide a lot of pulling power if Vic could just lift the bow enough to free it. If that didn't work, he was willing to bet Vic would figure something out. There was also the issue of Shauna's gunshot wound. Keith needed to get her to the hospital in Lafayette. He was sure he could get them to treat her if he took her there himself, and from the sound of it, if she didn't get that hand fixed correctly, it would never heal properly and she might never regain full use of it. As he thought of all this, he suddenly remembered that Vic had plans to leave later that morning. If he didn't catch him first, they would have to wait for tomorrow to even get his opinion on how to proceed. Waiting on Eric was going to make him too late.

"I don't know what could be keeping him so long," Keith told Jonathan. "It's not like he could get lost in St. Martinsville. If he went to the sheriff's office, he would quickly see that it's boarded up and no one is there anymore. I think we ought to go look for him, Jonathan. I don't like the idea of my dad being stranded down there in the marsh on that boat. I want to get down there today, without fail. We need to catch my brother-in-law before he leaves this morning and see if he'll help. He's got a boat that I'm pretty sure will do the job."

"But what if Eric comes back and I'm not here? What will he think then? I know he'll be pissed at me for not waiting like he told me to."

"He'll see my patrol boat, so he'll know I've been here. Besides, we can leave a note in the dinghy for him too, to let him know we're looking for him. Come on. We'll take Lynn's Cherokee. We'll run over to the sheriff's office first. Maybe we'll pass him on the way."

Keith wrote the note himself, explaining what they were going to do. He hoped Eric would recognize his signature, but even if he didn't, he would have no reason to doubt it. He didn't quite know what to make of Eric being delayed so long, but he figured that since his brother was heading for the sheriff's office in St. Martinsville, that's where he should look first. But just after they turned west off the road leading from his house, Keith and Jonathan came upon the scene of some kind of incident. John Lowery, one of Keith's distant neighbors who lived farther north on the bayou, was standing by the side of the road talking to another fellow that Keith had seen before, but whose name he didn't know. John's truck was pulled off on the shoulder, as was the one the other man was driving, and they were looking at two vehicles apparently abandoned in the middle of the lanes. One of them was a red Toyota Matrix, and Keith could see that it had been shot up by the flat tire and shattered window glass and windshield. The truck parked beside it was a Ford F150 pickup that didn't appear to be damaged.

"Damn, dude! I wonder what happened here?" Jonathan said.

"I don't know, but I need to try and find out." Keith pulled over and got out of the Jeep. He could now see a body in the grass behind the car and another one inside, slumped over the steering wheel, a jacket draped over the head and shoulders.

"What happened here, John?" Keith asked as he walked closer.

"I don't know, but there's three dead. Don't recognize any of them, but there's Louisiana plates on the car and the truck."

Keith saw the third body now; face down at the edge of the woods.

"Did you find any weapons?"

"Nope. If they had any, whoever killed them must have taken them. We were just talking about it, trying to figure out what happened."

"You haven't seen anybody else go by have you, maybe in my Tahoe with the markings?"

"Nope. Did somebody steal it? Do you think they were involved in this?"

"No, not at all. My brother took it, looking for me. I think he went to the office. That's where we're headed now, trying to track him down. I'll see if we can figure out who these men were, and then I'll have them picked up. That's about all I can do right now."

Keith checked the bodies and only found a wallet on one of the men; the one that had died at the edge of the woods from what was probably a pistol round to the face. The driver's license in it showed his age to be 26, and that he had a New Orleans street address. There was cash in the wallet too; mostly useless now, but still, Keith wondered why whoever did this didn't take it since the other two had no wallets on them. From the looks of the other guy beside the truck, with two in the chest and one in the head, it almost looked like an execution killing. Whatever their motivation, the killers had been thorough. The victim in the driver's seat of the car had been shot in the head at close range with a shotgun.

"What are you gonna do, man?" Jonathan asked, when Keith returned to the Jeep. "Are you going to have to look for whoever did this, since you're a deputy?"

"No. I imagine they're long gone by now. Those men have been dead for at least a couple of hours. We haven't had the resources to hunt down criminals in weeks. Most of the men in our department are dead, including the sheriff. I almost lost another partner and good friend in a shootout just a couple of days ago. He was badly wounded, but I got him to the hospital in Lafayette and they got the bullet out."

"Is that the same hospital you plan to take Shauna to?"

"Yep. It's the only one in the whole region that's open, as far as I know, and they're not able to treat everybody. They'll make an exception for her, I think, just because they're doing all they can for law enforcement and their families."

"Yeah, I can see that. People need you guys. It's so crazy everywhere now."

Keith was already driving away from the scene of the roadside shooting as they talked. It was so frustrating to him that he couldn't prevent such things, but in the big scheme of things now, three men dead was nothing. Hundreds of citizens of his parish had been killed in the bridge attacks and various smaller shootings, including the single-victim sort like the one the other day when Mr. Patel was murdered in front of his store.

As he followed the road to St. Martinsville, Keith wondered if the killing behind them happened before or after Eric passed that way in the dark hours of morning. It didn't make sense that he hadn't returned to the house yet. He'd had plenty of time to go and see that no one was around at the sheriff's office and Keith didn't think Eric would have any other ideas of where to look for him. If Bart had told him where Lynn's parents lived over on the west side of the basin, Eric hadn't said anything to Jonathan about it. All Keith knew to do was ride by the sheriff's office and check there. Then he would go to Vic's and try to catch him before he left to go to his aunt's.

A half hour later, after cruising through town and looking everywhere for a glimpse of the white Tahoe with no luck, Keith and Jonathan were pulling up to Vic's, and Keith was relieved to see that he was still home.

"So that's you're brother-in-law's boat?" Jonathan asked, seeing the big fishing vessel tied to the dock beside the waterfront house. "It's a lot bigger than I pictured it."

"Yeah, that's it. It's a shrimper. I think it's about 45-feet long, but Vic can tell you for sure. What do you think?"

"I think it could totally move *Dreamtime,* dude! It's got those big outrigger booms and the winches. It looks a lot like those two boats that followed us out in the Gulf to attack us. Is that your brother-in-law's truck? You didn't tell me he was a deputy too."

"He's not. That's Greg's truck, my partner that's in the hospital. Come on, let's go talk to Vic and tell him what's going on."

Ten minutes later, Keith and Jonathan were on the deck of Vic's *Miss Anita,* Jonathan describing the predicament the schooner was in and pointing out its approximate location on Vic's charts of the river entrance.

"All we can do it try it, bro. If it don't work, we'll have to figure out something else, but I think like you said, with your boat pulling her from the stern and me lifting as much as I can by the bow, she might slide back off it the way she went up on it. Only thing is, the tide's gonna be falling again by the time we get there, so we can't afford to wait." Vic was looking at his tide tables for the area.

"What's the range?" Keith asked.

"Not much. Maybe a foot and a half, but that's still enough to make a difference, especially at full low. If we hurry we oughta get there before it's halfway down. All we can do is try. I'm willing if you are, bro. Aunt Francine's house can wait! I'll just need to replace the fuel it takes to run down there and back."

"We'll take care of that," Keith said.

"Eric will pay for it, I promise you that," Jonathan said. "If there's somewhere to get some diesel, he's going to want to top off the tanks and Jerry cans on the schooner too."

"We'll work it out. But like I said, we don't need to wait. Anything could happen down there, and the sooner we get this done the better. It won't take me but a couple hours to get ready, and I'll start heading that way."

"Great!" Keith said. "I guess we'll see you down there. Don't forget your shotgun. You'd better bring a rifle too. There are some lonely stretches of river between here and there, as you well know."

"Don't worry about me, bro. I've got it covered."

Keith felt good about their prospects for rescuing the schooner after talking to Vic. As he and Jonathan drove back to his house, he kept his eyes open, looking for the Tahoe but they passed only a couple of other vehicles before they reached the scene of the shooting, which was just as it was when they left it.

"So they'll just come pick them up and haul them off to be buried?" Jonathan asked.

"Yep, it's all we can do. I'm hanging on to any I.D.s I find in case something comes up later, but that's about it. Case closed as far as I'm concerned."

When they turned into the driveway, Keith was disappointed and surprised to see that Eric still hadn't returned. He sent Jonathan over to check the dinghy and see if the note he'd left there was still in it, just to be sure, but it was. It didn't make any sense that Eric would just disappear like that. *Where in the hell could he have gone that would take him so long to get back?* Keith looked at his watch. It was already nearly 9 a.m. It was a long way down the river and the high tide was already in and would soon start going back out. Keith hated the idea of leaving without him, but Eric was a grown man, not to mention a badass former Navy SEAL and contractor. He could take care of himself and Keith would just have to see him later. He told Jonathan to revise the note to let him know they'd gone on downriver, and then the two of them boarded his patrol boat and left.

Seventeen

ERIC BAILED OUT OF the SUV so fast when he saw the shotgun pointed his way that he didn't have time to grab the M4. It didn't matter though. He had come upon the vehicles in the road so quickly when he rounded the bend that he was quite close by the time he stopped. His Glock 19 was already in hand as he crouched low beside the driver's side fender, the man firing the shotgun too confused by the flashing lights to even realize he'd left the vehicle. Eric centered the red dot from the Trijicon RMR sight on the shooter and dropped him with a smooth double-tap to the chest. When the other guy realized what was happening, he let go of the girl and dove for the weeds on the shoulder of the road. Eric stood to get in position to fire over the hood of the vehicle as the man tripped and then drew a pistol of his own as he crawled for the cover of the trees. When he raised it to fire, Eric put the dot between his eyes and squeezed off a single round, putting him away instantly and permanently. The terrified girl had dropped to a low crouch behind the tailgate of the truck by then, screaming and covering her ears against the noise of the gunshots. When Eric was certain there were no more threats, he reached back into the Tahoe and flipped off the blue lights. Then he walked towards the pickup. The first man he'd shot was still wheezing and gasping as he lay there dying from a ventilated chest. Eric put an anchoring shot through the side of his head to silence him, and then bent and picked up the shotgun he'd dropped. When he turned his attention back to the girl, she was practically hysterical, and now Eric could see why. The driver's side window of the Toyota car had been shot out. The headlights from the Tahoe revealed someone slumped over the steering wheel, and Eric saw with a glance that it was a man with part of his head missing. It didn't take a genius to figure out that the man from the truck had shot him at close range with the 12-gauge Eric had just picked up.

"Are you hurt?" he asked the girl, who was now frantically pulling open the rear door of the car, crying out for someone she clearly expected to find there.

Eric hadn't noticed, but there was a child lying in the back seat, and from the way she was acting, the child was obviously hers. He could now see that she was perhaps a little older than he'd first thought, maybe in her mid to late twenties. The child wasn't moving, and Eric saw that it was a little boy of about four or five.

"Is he your son? Was he shot too?"

The young woman turned to look back at Eric. "Yes, he is. They didn't shoot him, they just shot Danny, but Sammy is going to die anyway if he doesn't get to a hospital! That's where we were going when those men saw us. Danny turned off at the exit back there hoping they would go on, but they followed us and then they just pulled up beside the car and started shooting! It happened right before you showed up. Thank God you're a policeman! You've got to help me!"

Eric didn't bother correcting her. She was still hysterical and seemed much more upset about whatever was wrong with the child in the back seat than she was about the dead driver of the car. "What's the matter with the boy? Is he hurt? Or sick?"

"He got bitten by a cottonmouth! We didn't know what was wrong with him at first. He started screaming just before we were about to go inside for the night. We'd been sitting out by the fire in the backyard after we cooked supper, like we always do ever since the hurricane. Sammy was playing over by the back porch nearby and then he started hollering and crying, and holding his left hand. We just thought he'd scraped it on a nail or something, but then after we took him inside and got a flashlight, we saw the bite marks. It started swelling up something awful and turning dark within minutes. Danny went back out there with the light to look around and sure enough, he found a snake coiled up in the bushes right next to the porch. He killed it with a piece of firewood, and when he looked closer at it with the light, he said it was definitely a cottonmouth. You know how poisonous those things are if you live around here."

Eric did know. Even though he didn't live here, he'd grown up in snake country and the cottonmouth was certainly one to be avoided. The bite wasn't usually fatal for adults, but much more likely to prove so for a small child, especially if anti venom wasn't available. Eric doubted it was, even if there were an open hospital to be found, which he also doubted. He looked into the back seat of the car where the woman was now stroking the child's head and talking to him. The boy looked unconscious, or close to it, appearing completely unresponsive.

"Where were you taking him? Surely there aren't any hospitals open, are there?"

"There's one in Lafayette. It's the only one I know of. We heard they had volunteer doctors and nurses helping people there. They're keeping it going on generators as much as they can, but we heard they've been turning a lot of people away too, because they're running out of medicine and supplies. It's Sammy's only chance though. He's getting a lot worse every hour. Look at that arm!"

Eric could see it now. The poor child's arm had ballooned to an enormous size and was horribly discolored. His chances of survival were probably slim, but seeing this young woman pleading, Eric couldn't say no. The attackers had shot out the back tire of the car before killing the driver. Without his help, she wasn't going anywhere and the boy would die on the side of the road just like the man behind the wheel.

"Okay," he said. "Let's get him into my truck. Actually, it's my brother's truck, and I'm *not* a law enforcement officer. And you'll have to tell me how to get there, because I'm not from around here and I don't know the way to the hospital in Lafayette. We'd better get going quick though, before someone comes along and sees this."

The woman was thanking him profusely as she picked up her small son and carried him to the SUV. While she was getting him situated, Eric collected the weapons from the two dead attackers and removed a wallet from the pocket of the driver of the car. Spotting a light jacket in the back seat, he threw it over the mess that had once been the man's head, and when he returned, he handed the wallet to the woman, who was in the back seat of the SUV with the boy. "You might want this. Was he your husband? The boy's father?"

"No. Sammy's father is dead."

She offered no further explanation regarding the driver and Eric didn't ask. She was badly shaken, but seemed calmer now that she knew he was going to take her and her son to the hospital. Eric still had questions he needed answers to though, in case the two men he'd shot weren't the only threat.

"Did you know those two guys? Did they follow you here from somewhere?"

"No. Like I told you, they saw us on the interstate. Hardly anybody drives on it anymore, especially not after dark. They were going real slow in the same direction we were and Danny had to pass them because we were in a hurry. When he got in the left lane to go around them, they sped up to the same speed we were going and started yelling something at us. Danny tried to slow down again but they wouldn't leave us alone, I think it was because they could see me in the car. He turned off at the first exit he saw and they were right behind us until we got on this road, and then they just started shooting."

Eric backed up and turned the SUV around. The shotgun blast had gone through the center of the windshield in a fairly tight pattern. He could see through the cracked glass as long as there wasn't oncoming traffic with glaring lights, but he doubted that would be an issue. He headed west, but had no intention of getting on the interstate, and hoped he could find an alternate route to Lafayette. He'd seen a sign earlier when he'd turned off to the south to go to St. Martinsville. Lafayette was west, but he wasn't sure just how far. He should have been back at Keith's by now, and he knew Jonathan would be getting anxious, wondering what was taking him so long. All of these little problems, like finding Keith or letting Jonathan know what was up would be non-issues if the damned cell networks were still working. People really took that stuff for granted before, and not just here in America. Eric had noted that the addiction to instantaneous and constant connection had become ubiquitous, even in developing nations. Now, when it was all taken away after everyone was so used to it, life without it was a real pain in the ass. He glanced in the rear-view mirror at the woman, who was holding her child, uncertain if he would survive long enough to even reach the hospital, where it was even more uncertain if they could do anything for him.

"How is he? It's Sammy, right?"

"Yes, that's right. He's about the same I think. Not any worse."

"Don't give up. We're going to get there. What about you? What's your name? I'm Eric. Eric Branson. My brother, Keith is the deputy that this truck belongs to. Do you live here in St. Martin Parish?"

"Oh, sorry. I'm Cynthia. No, we live in St. Landry Parish."

"Is that nearby, Cynthia?"

"Yes, it's just to the north, on this side of the river. We had barely gotten onto I-10 when we saw that truck ahead of us. You said you're not from around here?"

"No. I came here looking for my brother." Eric continued on through the intersection where he'd turned before. "Do you think this is the right road? Can you find the hospital when we get to Lafayette?"

"I think so. Just keep going and I'll recognize stuff when we get closer. I used to go there a lot, but always from I-10 and never when it was this dark, with the lights all out."

Eric nodded and drove on in silence until Cynthia asked him another question.

"You said you're not a law enforcement officer. How did you know what to do back there? You shot both of those men with just a pistol before they could do anything."

"I've had some practice. We live in a dangerous world—especially now. It pays to be prepared."

"I just want to thank you, then. You didn't have to help us. I thought you did it because you had to... because you were a cop... but you could have just gone on by...."

"Not really. I saw what they were going to do to you. I can't help everyone, but I haven't had any luck finding my brother, so I wasn't in a particular hurry to just go back to his house and wait." Eric briefly told her about his predicament with the boat, and how he needed his brother's help to get it free.

When they reached Lafayette, Cynthia recognized familiar buildings and streets. She made a couple of mistakes telling Eric where to turn, but after doubling back and driving around a bit more, she spotted the hospital she was looking for, and Eric saw that there were indeed some lights on. The only entrance that wasn't blocked off by rows of vehicles was the emergency room, and as they approached Eric saw two guards armed with rifles standing behind a barricade that had been built in front of the entrance. He rolled down his driver's side window and slowly eased forward, hoping the sheriff's department emblem clearly visible on the door would give him an in. One of the guards stepped forward, rifle in hand, while the other stayed back to cover him. The man was focused on Eric's face as he drew closer.

"I thought you might be the deputy that brought his partner in the other night after the shooting, but I see you're not. He was in a different truck too. Can I help you?"

Eric briefly forgot why he was here when he heard the mention of a deputy and a shooting. *Could it be Keith? Was that why he wasn't home?* "Who was shot? A St. Martin Parish deputy? Do you know his name? Did he survive?"

"Sorry, I don't know his name, but as far as I know, he's still inside. His partner came back to check on him, I think."

"This is my brother's truck. He's the deputy, not me. I'm here because I have a snakebite victim in the back—a small child that's going to die if he doesn't get help. Will they see him?"

The guard turned to his partner and signaled him to go check. "I think they will, considering your brother's a deputy. Just hold on just a minute and we'll see. How did the kid get on a snake?" Eric told him but his mind was still on the wounded deputy. As soon as the guard returned, followed by a couple more men rolling a gurney who took Sammy out of the back seat, Eric locked up the truck and followed them inside. Cynthia thanked him again for his help and Eric wished her luck and said he would check on them before he left. The orderlies told him where to go to inquire about the wounded officer, and a couple minutes later, Eric tapped lightly on the door to the room and stepped inside. A red-headed man who looked to be in his early fifties looked up at him from where he was lying in the hospital bed, his face puzzled as Eric clearly wasn't a doctor or nurse.

"I'm sorry to disturb you," Eric said. "I thought you might be my brother when they said there was a wounded deputy in here."

"As far as I know, I don't have a brother," the man replied. He sounded weak, but he grinned as if he found that funny.

Eric smiled back. "Maybe you know him anyway though. You are with the St. Martin Parish Sheriff's Department, right? His name is Keith Branson."

The man's eyes lit up. "Keith? You're Keith's brother? I've heard all about you from him then! The name's Eric, right?"

"Yeah, that's right. Do you know where Keith is? Have you seen him?"

"Yeah, he was just here when I woke up. I don't know what time it was when he left, but I'm sure it wasn't more than about an hour ago. He's the one that brought me here. I'd be dead right now if not for him. I made a stupid mistake that got me shot. Keith covered for me though and drove me here when it was over. He wasn't expecting you, but he was going to look for your father today. It's Bart, right? Keith got a call from him on the VHF but he couldn't get back in touch with him. He was going down the river today to look for him there."

Eric felt a huge sense of relief, knowing that Keith was okay and that he'd just left this very room. He had to be on his way home then, they'd simply missed each other. He was willing to bet that Keith was probably already there now, talking to Jonathan. Helping Cynthia out of that fix and then driving her here had taken some time, but it didn't matter now, because he would soon see Keith and tell him exactly what was going on. He did want to know one more thing before he saw him though.

"Uh, do you know Keith's wife, Lynn?" Eric asked the deputy, whom he now knew was named Greg Hebert. "I saw something through the window at Keith's house. Did she die?"

"Unfortunately, yes. She was killed in the terror attack we had on the bridge at the time when people were evacuating because of the hurricane. It's been rough on your brother, as you can imagine. He was out working the river, checking on folks in the more remote areas to make sure they knew about the storm. He got to the bridge after it was over. We've had a lot going on around here, but that day was the worst of it." Greg went on to fill Eric in on the details of the attack.

"I know you probably don't feel like talking, and I can ask Keith more about it when I see him, but how in the hell did things come to this so fast in this country?"

"Man, I don't know. It's crazy though. I know you've seen it in other places. Keith told me all about your work, or what he knew of it, which probably isn't the half of it, right? Anyway, we're reduced to almost nothing as far as enforcement over there in St. Martin Parish. There hasn't been another big attack like that one since the hurricane, but there's still trouble and we can't be there for most of it. People are on their own now with no safety net, and plenty of them are managing just fine, and minding their own business, but desperation has driven a lot of them to things they wouldn't have considered before. That's how I got shot. Keith and I were clearing a store after armed looters killed the owner and holed up in there. The doctor says I'm going to be okay though. I hope so, because I need to get back out there and get to work."

Eric told Greg about the incident on the road that very morning that brought him here to the hospital. "I hope that kid makes it, but I'm not betting on it."

"You did a good thing, killing those thugs. I wish you could hang around here and help us take out some more of them. We could sure use a pro like you, but I don't imagine that's why you came here."

Eric told him that it wasn't, and that he had to get to Colorado to find Megan ASAP. He thanked Greg for all the info and told him he hoped to see him again before he left the area. When he left the room, he headed back to the emergency room area, where he found Cynthia talking to a man he presumed to be a doctor.

"They had the anti-venom!" she told Eric. "This is Dr. Taylor. He thinks it's going to work. Thanks to you, we got here in time!"

"We may not be able to save that arm though," the doctor told Eric. "It depends on how bad the tissue damage is. Cottonmouth venom is a neurotoxin that often causes severe necrosis in the extremities if enough of it is injected by the bite. I can tell you that due to Sammy's age and small size, he wouldn't have survived it without anti-venom."

"And without your hard work and dedication, Doctor Taylor. What you people are doing here is above and beyond, considering the present situation."

When the doctor excused himself to go see about another patient, Cynthia caught Eric off-guard with an unexpected request just as he was about to leave.

"You're not going back the way we came are you? Back towards the place where they shot Danny?"

"I've got to go by there, yeah. It's the only way I know to get back to my brother's."

"I hate to ask you this, but could you do me a huge favor? I don't want to leave Sammy here, but I need to let my parents know what happened. They live just a few miles from where we were staying at Danny's, and they come by everyday to check on us because they are super close to their only grandson. Word is going to get back to them about Danny being found dead in his car, and they are going to be worried sick wondering what happened to Sammy and me. They don't know about the snakebite because we didn't have time to go tell them. With no phones working or anything, I can't call them, and I don't have a way to get back out there."

"Well, I can drive you there, or I can go tell them where you are, I suppose."

Cynthia threw her arms around him and gave him a hug. "Thank you so much, Eric! You are too kind! I don't want to leave Sammy here because he's not out of the woods with this yet. But if you can take them a message, that would be wonderful."

Eric left the hospital with a note for Cynthia's parents in his pocket and directions to their house written on another piece of paper. He drove east into the light of the rising sun as it was just clearing the tops of the trees, thinking about how long all of this was taking. In order to deliver Cynthia's message, he had to go north of I-10 and then make several zigzagging turns on a series of back roads that roughly paralleled the river basin. It took him nearly two hours out of his way to get there and back to Keith's driveway. When he checked his watch as he was pulling in, he saw that it was 0930 and he immediately noticed that the Jeep Cherokee had been moved. It was now pulled up closer to the house, parked next to the sawhorses and lumber he'd seen there in the dark. Keith had to be back, because the steering of the Jeep had been locked.

Eric didn't see either Keith or Jonathan though, and when he got out and walked up to the house where he could see the dock out back, he didn't see a boat tied up there. He called their names and climbed the steps to check the house. No one was inside. If Keith had been back here, and Eric knew he must have, since that Jeep had been moved, he had already left again, apparently taking Jonathan with him. Eric wasn't sure what to make of it, until he descended the steps and went to check that the dinghy was still there where he and Jonathan had hidden it in the cattails. The note folded up and tied around the throttle of the outboard where Eric couldn't miss it explained everything. They didn't wait on him because Keith had arranged to meet a larger boat at the schooner that could possibly pull it off the wreck. Eric's side trip to Lafayette and then to Cynthia's parents' house had caused him to miss his ride, but that was okay. He'd saved her life and her little boy's as well, and he still had the dinghy, so he wasn't really stuck, but he did need gas for the outboard. Jonathan should have thought to tell Keith that, but he probably forgot about it and Keith had other things on his mind. That wasn't a problem though. He was sure Keith wouldn't mind if he siphoned some out of one of the vehicles. He grabbed the portable 6-gallon tank and walked back up to the house to look for a hose.

Eighteen

KEITH REGRETTED HE COULDN'T wait a little longer for Eric, but after what Vic said about the tide cycle, he knew they had to leave without delay if they were to have any hope of freeing the schooner today. There were only so many hours of daylight available, and it was a long way just to get down there to the lower reaches of the river. Vic would be heading out soon, but Keith knew it would take him longer to get there. Even though they couldn't accomplish the task without him, Keith wanted to go on ahead and check on Bart and the rest of his crew. He didn't like the idea of them being stranded in such an exposed location, and when he got there they could start making preparations for Vic's arrival later. Thinking about all that, Keith dismissed any second thoughts he had about waiting longer for Eric. He would come along anyway as soon as he returned to the house and found the note they'd left in the dinghy.

Learning that Eric was here, was of course a much bigger surprise to Keith than even the radio call from his father had been. Jonathan had filled him in on Eric's plans for getting

Megan, and about how Bart thought it might be a good idea for Eric to try and travel part of the way north and west by way of the river, working the fuel barges. Keith wasn't fully convinced that was the best option though, and he thought of another idea he would suggest to Eric when he saw him. It would be a faster way to reach Colorado while still keeping off the most dangerous roads. That was a discussion for later though, after the more pressing issues of dealing with the grounded schooner and Shauna's gunshot wound. It gave him something to think about during the long run downriver though, as it was mostly too noisy at the speeds he was running to talk much to Jonathan.

They were below Morgan City and in the salt marsh estuary of the lower Atchafalaya two hours later. Both of them were anxiously looking around that last bend when suddenly, they came into view of the schooner in the distance. From far away it was a strange-looking sight, listing to one side, as it was, the masts down in the horizontal position in their tabernacles. Keith would have thought it an abandoned wreck at first glance if he'd seen it without knowing what it was. Jonathan had told him that the radio calls he'd received from Bart had been made when the masts were up, with the antenna atop the taller mainmast. That's why there hadn't been any more calls after that first afternoon, but the radio would work fine at close range even without the tall antenna. Keith slowed and hailed *Dreamtime* on Channel 16 before he got within a quarter mile. Jonathan had already told him Bart would be keeping watch with his M1-A, and Keith knew what kind of marksman the old man was. It wouldn't do to go speeding up there unannounced, regardless of how anxious Keith was to see him. His transmission was a repeat of the replies that failed to reach him the other day, when the range was much greater.

"Vessel calling St. Martin Parish S.O., this is St. Martin Parish S.O., Deputy Branson. I have visual contact and will be approaching from upriver, off your starboard bow."

This time Keith got an immediate reply. Bart said later he had seen their boat coming and sure enough had gone below to get his rifle when the radio broke silence. By the time Keith and Jonathan pulled up to within speaking distance, Bart, Shauna, Daniel and Andrew were all on deck to greet them.

"I think you'll be in the clear if you tie up on our port side, son. I believe it's a little deeper there."

"I see that what Jonathan here told me is right. It look's like you're in a hell of a fix, Dad."

"I wasn't steering when it happened! Your Navy officer brother was! Where the hell is he? Why isn't he with you? And where is the dinghy?"

Keith filled him in briefly as he tied off and Jonathan climbed aboard. "I guess he'll be along eventually. The good news is that I've got help coming, Dad. My brother-in-law,

Vic, has a 45-foot shrimp trawler with outrigger booms. If he can get close enough, he thinks he can give us the lift Eric said it's going to take to get off of this mess. You can see I've got twin 150s on my patrol boat. I can provide a lot of pulling power from the stern at the same time. I think it'll work."

"That's good to hear, son. Speaking of your brother-in-law, how is Lynn? Did y'all make it all right through the hurricane? What about all the other trouble? Has it slacked up or gotten worse?"

Keith had known it wouldn't take long for Bart to ask about Lynn. He was very fond of his daughter-in-law, as he was of Shauna, evident by the fact that she was here with him along with her new husband and stepson. It was hard talking about it, especially since this was the first time after all those weeks Keith had been able to even tell anyone in his immediate family Lynn was gone. He told him what happened after he and Jonathan had boarded the schooner and sat down with everyone. He also told his father and Shauna how glad he was to see family again, at a time when he really needed them. "I'm looking forward to seeing Eric again too. Him coming here with you was the last thing I ever expected."

Keith had a look at Shauna's hand while they were waiting on Vic, and told her about the hospital in Lafayette. "I can take you there as soon as we get done here. My partner's truck is parked at Vic's so we can leave straight from there. We won't be able to get the schooner to my house anyway. The hurricane blew down a lot of trees around there, and there's still some in the water we haven't cleared out enough for larger vessels to pass. There's an empty dock at the house next to Vic's though, and I'm sure he can work out something with his neighbor to let us tie it up there."

"I'm surprised to hear there's a hospital open at all," Bart said.

"Lafayette was on the west side of the hurricane, so they weren't hit quite as hard there. It's also a small city, so it wasn't on anyone's radar for all the mayhem that's been going on in bigger places. The bridge over the swamp was a special case I guess. Some of the protesters got the bright idea several months back to try and stop traffic there by standing in the middle of it. It worked until the guns came out, but unfortunately, someone somewhere else was paying attention. The real terrorists took the bridge idea and ran with it, taking it to a whole different level."

"I'm so sorry about Lynn," Shauna said. "I can't imagine how hard this has been on you, Keith."

"I think what happened there is what we've been seeing in a lot of places, Bart said. Whether they are Islamic jihadists, commie anarchists or agitators trying to start a race war to bring down the country, they're all sorta borrowing from each other's playbook for their tactics. I suppose they all have a common enemy, and that enemy is a country they all hate with equal passion, even if not for the same reasons. Just like they hate the regular folks that are trying to hold it together. I don't know what the solution is, son."

"Me either, Dad. But we've about lost our entire sheriff's department in St. Martin Parish. I'm still doing what I can, but it's never enough. Just this morning, Jonathan and I came upon another roadside ambush. Three men dead just a few miles from my house. And this is a parish where in my whole career we didn't see a dozen murders before this year."

Their conversation was interrupted by another radio call. It was Vic, calling to let them know he was almost there.

Bart glanced at his watch and looked over the side at the water level. "Good thing he's here. It's down from peak but we might have time before it gets too low if we hurry."

When Vic arrived on site with his *Miss Anita,* it was soon apparent to everyone what an expert boatman he was. He first anchored just downstream of the stranded schooner so he could assess the situation. Keith picked him up in his boat and using his depth sounder they surveyed the bottom in the immediate vicinity to ensure there weren't any other obstructions they might run afoul of when positioning the trawler.

"I wish Eric were here," Keith said to Vic. "He's the expert diver. I don't exactly know what we're dealing with under there. Just what Jonathan told me that Eric saw."

"I can check it out for you if you want me to," Jonathan said. "I'm not an expert, but I've used a mask and snorkel in Florida. Like Eric said though, the water's so murky here you can't see anything. You have to go by feel."

"I don't think it's necessary to try and mess around under there near that old wreck," Vic said. "It's too dangerous if you can't see. You might get hung up and drown, bro. Maybe if you just check around in the area just in front of the schooner and be sure we didn't miss anything we might hit. As long as I can get in position abeam of the bow without running aground myself, I can get one of the outrigger booms over it. I'll put the other one out opposite and we'll get some anchors on it so she won't list too far with the weight. I think it's gonna work as long as we've got enough water. It looks like just a little bit of a lift is all you need."

It took another hour to get all this done and by then, the tide was noticeably lower. When they were ready, Bart was at the helm of the schooner and Jonathan and Daniel were aboard the *Miss Anita* helping Vic. Keith had rigged a long towline from one of *Dreamtime's* anchor warps to the stern of his patrol boat, and was standing by 200 feet downriver, waiting for the signal to pull from astern. Shauna and Andrew were with Bart in the cockpit, ready to help him anyway they could.

At first, Keith didn't think it was going to work at all. When Vic loaded up the big winch for the steel cable they'd attached to *Dreamtime's* samson post, he wasn't sure if the post was going to be ripped out or if the trawler would simply move too much to get any purchase, but he knew something had to give. He eased his own engines into gear and took up all the slack in the towline, gradually increasing power until the heavy braided nylon was fully stretched and ready to pull. The schooner gradually began to slide back, and then the weight of the keel apparently found another place to break through the wreckage beneath it and the hull slowly began to settle back to level. This wasn't good, because now with the keel straight down, there was more draft to deal with and it probably wasn't going to budge.

But Bart said they could remedy that by getting an anchor out into the nearby marsh, attached to the halyards from the mast, so they could heel it back over a bit like it was before and then try again. The problem with that solution was that both masts were still down, which meant they had to scramble to get one of them stepped again so they could set the kedge from the halyard before the tide fell too much. That took nearly another hour, and then Jonathan volunteered to wade into the muddy marsh with the anchor. When they heeled the schooner back over to between 10 and 15 degrees using a tackle connected to the windlass, the hull finally began to slide aft with the pull from Keith's boat and then suddenly, *Dreamtime* was floating free. The mast would have to be lowered again for the trip upriver, but Bart deemed the vessel seaworthy after checking carefully in all the nooks and crannies of the bilge for leaks and other signs of damage and finding nothing.

"I think we're good to go," Bart said. "If there was any damage to the hull, it was only superficial. The keel is probably gouged up pretty bad, but I'm pretty sure the prop and the rudder didn't hit anything, so no issues there. The only problem we've got now is that there are only a few hours of daylight left. We won't have time to get much past Morgan City before dark at our cruising speed."

Bart had dropped *Dreamtime's* main anchor just downstream of the submerged wreck so he could do the inspection. Vic was still anchored just upriver, and Keith had pulled his patrol boat alongside the schooner after picking up Jonathan and Daniel from the trawler.

"Vic knows this river like the back of his hand," Keith said. "He says it won't be a problem to navigate it in the dark. He's not worried about hitting hurricane debris out in the channel, because the towboats have been using it since the storm. If you stay directly in his wake you'll be fine. I know he'd rather head on back than anchor overnight down here. If you're comfortable with it, I think we should let him make the decision."

"Oh I agree. He came all the way down here to help us. I don't have a problem trusting that he knows the river. I just can't figure out what would keep Eric so long. I hate to leave without him, but I guess maybe we'll run into him along the way."

"I can't figure it out either, Dad. All I can think of is that he must have run into some kind of trouble. There's no other reason he shouldn't have been back to the house before we left. And even though he missed us, there's no reason he shouldn't have had time to get back down here by now. I'll keep an eye out for the dinghy on my way to Vic's. Maybe I'll spot him and save him the trouble of going all the way down until he meets you. I just hope he doesn't get off on one of the side channels trying to take a shortcut or something. I'd hate for him to miss us and get all the way down here and find us gone. I don't know how much gas he's carrying, but he sure won't find any around here.

"Not enough," Jonathan said. "He said we'd have to get some from you or somebody else upriver just to have enough to get back down here."

"Well, I doubt lack of fuel is what's keeping him now. If he made it back to the house, he would know to get some out of one of my vehicles or the bikes, even if he doesn't find my underground storage tank."

Keith was torn about going on ahead of the two boats, but it didn't make a lot of sense for him to spend hours chugging up the river at eight knots or less when he had those big engines and plenty of fuel in his patrol boat. Shauna's hand wasn't a matter of life or death at this point, but she was still in a lot of pain and the sooner he got her to the hospital, the better. He knew he could make it to Vic's before dark in his much faster boat, and with Greg's truck waiting there, he could drive her to the hospital tonight. Bart encouraged him to go ahead with that idea. Shauna tried to argue, insisting that she had waited this long and she could wait longer, but Daniel and Andrew urged her to go too."

"You and Andrew could go on along with them if you want to," Bart said to Daniel. I've got Jonathan to spell me at the helm, and Vic knows where he's going, so we don't have to worry about navigation. Go on with her and Keith and we'll see you all tomorrow."

Keith could tell that Daniel wanted to do just that. It was natural that he would want to accompany his wife to the hospital, but he looked at her and then back at Keith and Bart and said they would stay to help with the boats. He said he knew Vic could use an extra hand aboard the *Miss Anita* to give him a break from the helm, and that he trusted that Keith was more than capable of getting Shauna to the hospital safely on his own, because he was trained and well armed and his boat was fast enough to evade most anyone they might encounter. Daniel hugged his wife and kissed her good-bye, and then Keith helped Shauna over the rail of the schooner and into his patrol boat, and the two of them sped away to the north.

* * *

Bart hadn't tried to convince them one way or the other, but after Keith and Shauna were gone he had to admit he was grateful that Daniel and Andrew were willing to stay and help. The two of them, especially Daniel, had come a long way since they left Florida, and in more ways than one. He had learned the importance of working together as a team and had finally come to understand that this situation was equally hard on everyone, and that there were no special cases. Bart was proud of both of them for remaining on board as dedicated members of the crew until *Dreamtime* was safely tied up in her new temporary berth next to Vic's.

When both vessels had their anchors up and were ready to go, Bart pulled just near enough alongside the *Miss Anita* for Jonathan to hop aboard. He would help out Vic while Daniel and Andrew remained on the schooner with Bart. This was going to make the long trip upriver easier on everybody, and when they started heading north, Bart couldn't have been any happier to leave that desolate expanse of marsh astern. After what he'd seen in Florida, and especially after their experience with the two boats that followed them out to sea from the barricade, the hours he'd spent stuck and helpless on that stranded boat seemed to drag on forever. Trouble would have found them if they'd been there long enough, Bart was sure of that, but now they were free and once again en route to their destination. Things were coming together, mostly as planned, but there was sadness too, as Bart followed Vic up the river, his thoughts returning to Keith and all that his youngest son had been through in recent weeks. Losing a wife was hard, as Bart knew all too well, and at Keith's age he shouldn't have to deal with that. Bart had known he would be facing trying times as a law enforcement officer dealing with the riots and violence, not to mention the aftermath of a major hurricane, but he hadn't expected to get that news. Bart had been looking forward to seeing his daughter-in-law almost as much as his son, but now he'd missed his chance. The happy reunion he'd looked forward to, being together with both of his boys at once for the first time in years, would be marred by Lynn's absence. He knew it could be worse though. With all the men Keith said they lost in his department, it was a wonder he too wasn't among the fallen.

Bart was also getting slightly concerned about Eric, but he still wasn't overly worried. Whatever had delayed him, he was confident Eric could handle it, but it was puzzling that he would be delayed so long. Talking to Jonathan about it, the kid certainly didn't get the impression that Eric was going to be gone much longer than it would take to drive to the sheriff's office and back. Something had diverted or detained him, and Bart couldn't help but wonder what that might be. He didn't get his answers until a few hours later.

They had passed under the low bridges at Morgan City just before sundown, and by the time it was fully dark, were motoring past heavily wooded banks on a lonely stretch of the Atchafalaya to the north. Bart saw Vic suddenly cut his speed, and he eased back his own throttle to keep from closing the gap between them. Andrew climbed up on the cabin top with the binoculars at Bart's suggestion, to see if he could see anything, and a moment later yelled that he saw a light flash on and then go off not far ahead on the river. This immediately made Bart nervous. Were they about to meet another towboat pushing barges like the one that had run them out of the channel before? An encounter like that at night would really be dicey, with an even greater risk of collision. Bart had hoped the tows wouldn't be running at night, and none had passed by the night they spent stranded in the marsh. But when he scanned the river where Andrew said he'd seen the light, there was nothing out there that he could see.

"It just flashed on for a second." Andrew said.

Bart knew Vic must have seen something too, and he was about to ask Daniel to give him a call on the radio when Andrew shouted again. "It's Eric! I can see the dinghy now!"

Bart saw that he was right. The dinghy was approaching them out of the dark from off to port. Eric slowed just before he reached them and expertly brought the inflatable alongside the schooner. "I see that Keith's plan worked!" Eric said, as he handed Bart a line. "I got the note he left, saying his brother-in-law had a boat that could do the job. Where is Keith now? Where's Jonathan?"

"Jonathan's on the trawler there with Vic," Bart said. "Keith went on ahead upriver with Shauna. He's taking her to the hospital in Lafayette to get that hand looked at. You didn't see them on your way down? Where in the hell have you been all day? We were expecting you to show up hours ago."

"It's kind of a long story, Dad. I already missed Keith and Jonathan because of what happened when I drove into town in his truck, but as it turned out, that wasn't the half of it. Let's get going and I'll tell you all about it on the way. I'll just tie the dinghy off and we can tow it. There's no sense taking the time to load it on deck right now. The sooner we can get that schooner someplace safe, the better."

"We've got a place to tie her up; at a dock next to the one where Vic keeps the trawler. Keith's patrol boat should be there when we get there. You'll see him in the morning, I'm sure."

"Good. Now I can make a plan to get to Colorado ASAP and get Megan. I want to leave without delay, too. I've seen enough here already to know that I can't afford to wait. I just hope I'm not already too late."

About the Author

SCOTT B. WILLIAMS HAS been writing about his adventures for more than twenty-five years. His published work includes dozens of magazine articles and twenty-two books, with more projects currently underway. His interest in backpacking, sea kayaking and sailing small boats to remote places led him to pursue the wilderness survival skills that he has written about in his popular survival nonfiction books such as *Bug Out: The Complete Plan for Escaping a Catastrophic Disaster Before It's Too Late*. He has also authored travel narratives such as *On Island Time: Kayaking the Caribbean*, an account of his two-year solo kayaking journey through the islands. With the release of *The Pulse* in 2012, Scott moved into writing fiction and has written several more novels with many more in the works. To learn more about his upcoming books or to contact Scott, visit his website: www.scottbwilliams.com

Made in the
USA
Monee, IL